CHOUCAS

AN INTERNATIONAL NOVEL

Zofia Nałkowska

TRANSLATED BY URSULA PHILLIPS

NIU Press
DeKalb, IL

Published by the Northern Illinois University Press, DeKalb, Illinois 60115
Manufactured in the United States using acid-free paper
Design by Shaun Allshouse

Library of Congress Cataloging-in-Publication Data
Nalkowska, Zofia, 1884–1954.
[Choucas. English]
Choucas / Zofia Nalkowska ; translated by Ursula Phillips.
pages cm
Summary: «English translation of a novel by Zofia Nalkowska, originally
published in serial form in 1926, and then in book form in 1927. Set in
a village in the Swiss Alps in the mid-1920s, the female narrator and her
male companion, both Polish, are staying at a pension-cum-sanitorium.
The focus is not on them as Poles but on the international community
and the interaction between the community of the sick and of the winter
sports› clientele who represent various nations»—Provided by publisher.
Includes bibliographical references.
ISBN 978-0-87580-707-2 (paperback) — ISBN 978-1-60909-160-6
(e-book)
I. Phillips, Ursula, translator. II. Title.
PG7158.N34C4613 2014
893. 8'536—dc23   2014007231

CHOUCAS

CONTENTS

ACKNOWLEDGMENTS

Translations of complex literary texts never happen sponta-
neously (or if they do, they do so at their peril) and always involve the assistance of many advisers. First I would like to thank
Hanna Kirchner, biographer of Zofia Nałkowska and editor of
the six published volumes of her diaries, for her advice on the
various editions of *Choucas*, for our discussions of the novel
in April 2012 and March 2013, and for reading an earlier draft
of my Introduction. I would also like to express my thanks to
the late Irena Wróblewska-Korsak and to Joanna Wróblewska-
Kujawska, Zofia Nałkowska's heirs, for permitting this translation project to be published. I am also deeply grateful to the two
anonymous reviewers of both the translation and Introduction
whose comments resulted in various improvements.

In addition I thank a number of other people who have supported me in the venture and with whom I have discussed
aspects of the novel, especially Włodzimierz Bolecki, who en-
couraged me to undertake the translation in the first place, and
Grażyna Borkowska, for also reading my Introduction. I am
greatly indebted to Dorota Hołowiak for her help in resolving
certain vocabulary problems in the original Polish.

Special thanks are due to Gagik Stepan-Sarkissian, librarian
of the Armenian Institute in London, who assisted in verifying
the references to the history and culture of Armenia, advised on
how Armenian names would be best rendered in English, and
identified the Armenian liturgical text as well as the source of the
quotations, allegedly from official Turkish documents relating to
the 1915/16 genocide of Armenians.

ACKNOWLEDGMENTS

I am most grateful to Corinne Fournier Kiss, Tibor Kiss and Jérôme Fournier, and Erika and Nick Panagakis for helping to identify the bird of the title as the Alpine chough, as well as to residents of Leysin, Switzerland—in particular Véronique Bernard, Helayne and Michel von May, and Steven Ott—for their help in finding specific places connected with Zofia Nałkowska's stay in 1925 and for providing information and materials on the history of the sanatoria town.

I remain eternally indebted to Łukasz Ossowski, librarian of the Institute of Literary Research of the Polish Academy of Sciences, for his assistance with materials not available to me in the UK. Finally, I thank my husband, Felix Corley, for his constant support and unflagging investigative spirit on location in Leysin.

INTRODUCTION

Ursula Phillips

Zofia Nałkowska (1884–1954) was one of the most out-
standing Polish writers and cultural figures of the first half of
the twentieth century, recipient of many prestigious literary
awards both before and after 1945. She is regarded as a pioneer
of the psychological novel in Polish, following Karol Irzykowski
(1873–1944) and Stefan Żeromski (1864–1925). Having drawn
inspiration in her early years from Nietszche, Schopenhauer, and
Bergson, her mature prose was more deeply influenced by the
psychological realism of Stendhal and Flaubert, Dostoevsky and
Proust. Her approach to human behavior, interhuman relations,
and personality formation, and to their portrayal in literature
may be said to anticipate the work of novelist and playwright
Witold Gombrowicz (1904–1969) (Kirchner 1984). In addition,
she was a significant voice promoting the visibility of women
in early-twentieth-century literature, alongside other prominent
Polish authors active between the two world wars, such as Maria
Dąbrowska, Pola Gojawiczyńska, Maria Jehanne Wielopolska,
Helena Boguszewska, Maria Kuncewiczowa, Wanda Melcer, Irena
Krzywicka, and others (Kraskowska 1999; Borkowska 2001b).

Daughter of well-known scholar, geographer, and critic
Wacław Nałkowski (1851–1911), she grew up in Warsaw in the
politically progressive atmosphere of her father's intellectual mi-
lieu, immersed in the literature of the Modernist fin-de-siècle,
and personally acquainted with leading Polish cultural figures of
the time. An admirer of philosopher and cultural critic Stanisław
Brzozowski (1878–1911), she was an advocate throughout her life
of liberal ideas, social tolerance, and humanitarian empathy with

victims of oppression and suffering. She was associated, for example, with the progressive literary group Suburb (Przedmieście, 1933–1937). After World War II she was a member of the official Commission for Investigating Nazi Crimes in Poland, an experience that found powerful literary expression in her collection of short prose *Medallions* (*Medaliony*, 1946).

During Nałkowska's lifetime, her native land—from 1795 to 1918 partitioned between three competing empires (Russia, Austria, and Prussia)—underwent a series of fundamental upheavals that formed the background, even if not explicitly stated, to most of her literary activity: the 1905 revolution as it affected the western *gubernias* of the Russian Empire, of which Warsaw was a part from 1815 until 1918; the First World War, the activity of patriotic legions fighting for Polish national independence on both sides of the conflict, and the establishment of the Second Republic of Poland after the war; the Polish-Soviet War of 1920; the attempts in the early 1920s to establish a parliamentary democracy; Józef Piłsudski's *coup d'état* in May 1926; the Nazi and Soviet invasions of September 1939; the Second World War; the Holocaust; the Warsaw Ghetto Uprising, 1943, and the Warsaw Uprising, 1944; the establishment of communist power in a postwar Polish state with drastically reconfigured geographic and ethnic boundaries. Also of fundamental importance to her consciousness was the political situation in Europe generally, as well as contemporary artistic and literary developments that were taking place in elite European intellectual and cultural circles, especially French, to whose legacy she aspired and with whom she established personal contacts.

Zofia Nałkowska began to write as a teenager, poetry initially, as well as in diaries, which were to accompany her throughout her writing career, with some interruptions, and which themselves became a significant formative element in her own self-creation as an author, even arguably literary works in their own right (Kirchner 2011, 789–826). The existence of these diaries, gradually published in six volumes under Hanna Kirchner's editorship, was not known when Nałkowska's novels and short stories first appeared.[1]

Her literary production spans early Modernism—known in the Polish context as the Young Poland (*Młoda Polska*) movement—and then the more realistically oriented psychological novel, especially following the outbreak of World War I and the occupation of Warsaw by the Germans. It is then when Nałkowska's focus switched from self to other people, to the "world beyond me," to public life and collective concerns, including the phenomenon and psychology of war itself (irrespective of its causes). Her earlier, pre-1914 period is dominated by her private intellectual and emotional development and self-creation as a woman. Her debut as a novelist came in 1906, when she published her first full-length prose fiction in book form—the three-part novel *Women* (*Kobiety*).[2] The theme of female internal life never left her, but from 1914 onward the focus shifted from narcissistic, Nietzschean individualism, and identity as a New Woman—celebrating empowered female sexuality and challenging traditional women's roles and motherhood in works such as *Contemporaries* (*Rówieśnice*, 1909), *Narcyza* (1910), *Snakes and Roses* (*Węże i róże*, 1915), the short story collections *Little Kitten or White Tulips* (*Koteczka czyli białe tulipany*, 1909) and *Mirrors* (*Lustra*, 1913)—to the trauma of war and occupation as it affected Poles and their striving to re-establish political independence—notably in the collection *Blood Secrets* (*Tajemnice krwi*, 1917) and the novel *Count Emil* (*Hrabia Emil*, 1920).

Her primary focus became—and would always remain—the sufferings of human society at large, transcending ethnic and cultural boundaries and culminating eventually in her most powerful existential statement, the novel about several generations of a family driven by the urge to self-annihilation entitled *The Impatient Ones* (*Niecierpliwi*, 1939). Her writing would become characterized above all by a profound humanitarian empathy with all living creatures, including animals (she published three sets of short stories devoted to human interaction with animals[3]), acutely aware of suffering—physical, psychological, and moral. The general impression that emerges from her work is of a sense of human consciousness being the highest instance and value, a consciousness whose assessment of human behavior is ultimately tragic (beyond or irrespective of any religious or ideological imperatives). It has even been argued that she was already psychologically prepared for what she witnessed during the Nazi occupation of Warsaw and, following that, in her postwar capacity as a member of the Commission for Investigating Nazi Crimes. This all merely confirmed what she had already concluded about human nature, as her motto to *Medallions* suggests: "People dealt this fate to people."[4] Grażyna Borkowska puts it this way:

> Her experiences as a woman left her several times on the edge of a precipice. The war, which was objectively terrible, brought nothing new to Nałkowska's inner perception of the world, nor did it change anything in her observation of herself or other people. Accustomed to an environment of existential pessimism, Nałkowska was internally prepared for the war. She knew how to survive war because she knew how to survive life. (2001b, 153)

I would like to suggest, first, that some of the human experiences Nałkowska heard about during her stay in Switzerland in 1925 contributed to this view of human nature and, second, that the sufferings of several of the female characters in her novel may reflect—at least partially—some of her own agonies as a woman. *Choucas* appeared in the middle of a series of novels written in the 1920s and 1930s, in which Nałkowska, a close witness as a result of her marriage to Jan Gorzechowski to the mechanisms of power and methods of enforcement of the newly independent state, captures the moral and practical dilemmas, ideological conflicts, and administrative chaos of those years of political and economic transition. The series includes three other novels—*The Romance of Teresa Hennert* (*Romans Teresy Hennert*, 1924), *Bad Love* (*Niedobra miłość*, 1928), and *Boundaries* (*Granica*, 1935)—and the short story collection *Walls of the World* (*Ściany świata*, 1931). *Choucas,* subtitled *An International Novel,* is not about Poland itself, but captures rather the tensions between various nations' perceptions of one another in the mid-1920s—prejudices based more on internalized, emotionally driven stereotypes than on any objective criteria, or even on ideological differences (Bolecki 2003). Following the post-First World War political reconfiguration of Europe, Nałkowska's narrator intuits the gravity of the potential consequences of such prejudices against a background of previous atrocity, displacement, or moral bankruptcy experienced by the novel's characters, many of whom were based on real people Nałkowska met in the sanatoria village of Leysin, Switzerland in 1925.

GENESIS OF THE NOVEL *CHOUCAS*

Nałkowska was married twice, first (in 1904) to minor poet, publicist, and later pedagogue Leon Rygier (1875–1948), and second (in 1922) to Jan Jur-Gorzechowski (1874–1948), whom Nałkowska had first met in 1916, who was a close associate of Józef Piłsudski, a renowned fighter for Polish independence, and a veteran of Piłsudski's legions. After 1918, in independent Poland, her future husband rose to the position of superintendent of the military police in Wilno (Vilnius). The couple lived first outside Wilno and then in Grodno (present-day Hrodna in Belarus)—where Jur proved to be a tough, politically committed but jealous man, who treated his wife sadistically. As Kirchner observes, "The first ten years of independent Poland would have for Zofia Nałkowska the face of Jan Jur-Gorzechowski" (2011, 181); the marriage lasted until 1929. It was in the company of Gorzechowski that she made the journey in 1925 to Leysin, the location that inspired the novel *Choucas*. The purpose of the visit was the treatment of Gorzechowski, who was suffering with bone tuberculosis in his left hand. Nałkowska herself was not a patient.

After her return to Grodno, Nałkowska, at some point before mid-September 1925, began work on the novel. On 19 September, she records in her diary, almost in passing, amid a passage describing the beauty of the local countryside she explores on horse-back, as well as her constant fears of her own ageing (she would be forty-one on 10 November) and impending deafness, the following: "And then I return, sit down at my desk, write a little of this thing about Switzerland" (1980b, 175). The next mention is on 13 November, when she records its completion: "I have been working a great deal recently, but that doesn't mean I've written a great deal. The rough drafts stacked separately make up a pile six times higher than the final manuscript lying beside them. Its title is *Choucas*" (1980b, 184). The next diary mention is nine months later on 24 August 1926: "I have written quite a lot, sitting here in Warsaw […] and still constantly *Choucas*" (192), suggesting she continued to tinker with it. On 30 August, she records its acceptance by the Warsaw journal *The Illustrated Weekly* (*Tygodnik Ilustrowany*), which was a relief to her from the financial perspective, but publication in serial parts was not a form of publication she necessarily welcomed. The passage also betrays some of Nałkowska's characteristic lack of confidence in her artistic abilities and the stressful intellectual and emotional effort involved in creative activity, even a certain tension between the impulse to write and a lack of desire:

> Ah, God, what a relief! I have completed *Choucas*, written for consecutive issues of "The Illustrated Weekly," in haste, in distress, traveling back and forth, in partying and in despair. Such a form of publishing, which cannot be interrupted, is a constant nervous torture, because one is not allowed to be ill, not allowed

not to make the deadline, not allowed *to be unable* to write [Z.N.'s emphases]. This is already my fourth, even my fifth book written according to this method. I cannot do it otherwise—mainly because I need the money, and perhaps also from lack of will. Oh, how I dislike writing, how I loathe terribly what I have written! In rare paroxysms of good humor, I unexpectedly discover some value in my books, but it never lasts. I once said, trying to explain my laziness: I would rather read Dostoevsky than write Nałkowska. (1980b, 195–96)[5]

Following acceptance by *The Illustrated Weekly,* she also sold it to a book publisher: "I am in Warsaw—trying during these past few days to sell my *Choucas.* At the present time it's a great and difficult task" (1980b, 204; the reference may well be to the period following Piłsudski's *coup d'état,* which had taken place on 12 May). On 1 October she says, "Despite all expectations, I have had two offers for *Choucas.* I have sold it to Gebethner, though not on the best terms and conditions" (214). Thus the novel appeared first in serial parts in *The Illustrated Weekly* (1926, numbers 3–36) and then shortly afterward in book form (December 1926), published by Gebethner and Wolff, also in Warsaw, according to her own diary record (19 January 1927). Although the title page of the edition has 1927, it was common practice for books published in the run-up to Christmas to have the date of the coming year: "In December my *Choucas* appeared and there have already been a few reviews" (1980b, 229).

The reviews, however, were not numerous, and mostly failed to appreciate the innovative style of the text, or its contents. It was seen by some critics as an apology for pacifism.[6] While Nałkowska's narrator certainly reveals the sufferings of her protagonists, and juxtaposes these with the unexamined prejudices of other characters, it would be misguided to assign to her an overtly pacifistic agenda, or any ideological role at all beyond the ethical, which itself cannot be reduced anyway here to anything more substantial than the expression of an empathic moral consciousness. Nałkowska's narrator primarily bears witness and remains unengaged in the debates between the other characters, while also exemplifying a characteristic feature of Nałkowska's prose: the field of vision and hence of narration is confined to what is visible, or accessible, to the narrator as an actor *in medias res*. In this novel we have a first-person narrator, neither all-knowing nor objective, struggling to understand whatever she observes from her limited perspective.

WHICH BIRDS?

What species of bird does Nałkowska refer to in her novel's title and text? Clearly, we are dealing with the French name of a particular Alpine bird, which the narrator and her companion enjoy feeding every day on the balcony of their room. From the text, we know that it has a yellow bill and red legs; and Nałkowska's narrator gives detailed information about its various calls, flight patterns, impressive aerodynamics, eating habits, social behavior, and habitat. The birds are obviously found at high altitude. She calls these birds *choucas*. The French word has the same form in the singular and plural. When she refers to the book in her diary she uses a plural verb, suggesting that she intends (in the title) the birds to be understood as plural, and this is also confirmed by her frequent use of the Polish alternative: *Szuki* (the Polonized form *szuka*, singular, also appears frequently in the novel's text). If one looks up the French term *choucas* in standard French-English dictionaries, the English equivalent is given as "jackdaw" (Polish: *kawka*). However, the descriptions given in the novel are not of jackdaws. The bird that Nałkowska describes in detail is the Alpine chough (*pyrrhocorax graculus*); her descriptions correspond to the information given in standard guides relating to this species, not to information given on the jackdaw (*corvus monedula*).[7] Nałkowska's narrator is aware that the birds are not jackdaws, and she distinguishes between the two species in the novel's text: "Choucas do not caw like jackdaws, but warble or shrill delicately, rather like the chirruping of our own swallows and swifts" (chapter 2).

The Alpine chough is common in the Swiss Alps and regularly distributed above the tree line, while the jackdaw is found at lower altitudes and is even relatively rare in the upper reaches of the Rhône valley, where the novel is set. The French term for the Alpine chough is *chocard à bec jaune* or *chocard des Alpes*. The birds described by Nałkowska are *chocards* not *choucas*. However, it is a common error among local nonspecialists to confuse the two species, misnaming *chocards* as *choucas*; *chochards* are frequently referred to by the local population as *choucas*. Hence Nałkowska merely repeats the popular name used by the local people whom she met.[8]

It is significant that Nałkowska's reception of the birds differs fundamentally from that of the locals. Nałkowska's narrator reacts to the birds positively, describing them as gentle and lovable. In chapter 2, for example, we have the following: "they are very peaceable. I never saw them fight among themselves with their yellow bills, even when several descended on the balcony at the same time and couldn't all reach the food"; and in chapter 6: "the birds' glistening forms fall out of the radiant cornflower-blue, cheerful, chirruping, well-adjusted, likeable." The narrator and her companion go to great lengths to prepare food for them, so they can observe and admire them at close quarters. Mentions of the birds by other characters in the novel are more ambiguous. While the narrator is transfixed by the grotesque, painted wooden souvenir choucas in a shop display (all shapes and sizes and colors, but entirely out of proportion with enormous bills and tiny bodies), other (male) characters find them humorous and compare them to Mademoiselle Hovsepian and Mademoiselle Alice (chapter 19). The narrator is taken aback at these comparisons, which have negative connotations, reflecting also how the men regard the two women. On a recent visit to the region, seeking myself similar souvenirs, I was unable to find any choucas (or: *chocards*) among the stacks of toy cows, chamois, marmots, bears and other Alpine fauna. I was assured by several local people that there was a reason for this: namely, the choucas are regarded as birds of ill omen. When they come down to the village for the winter months in search of food—their very presence a sign of bad weather higher up—they even fight other birds, such as magpies. Whilst Nałkowska's narrator describes how a feeding choucas may sometimes become angry and shove another bird off the balustrade (chapter 2), she generally perceives them as peaceable and develops a genuine affection for them. What then are we to make of the novel's closing scene describing a flock of choucas circling over the valley? A nostalgic farewell to the narrator's beloved companions on a par with her leave-taking of her human friends? Or a warning of impending doom hanging over Europe—a finale indeed in tune with the novel's main theme?

THE THEME OF THE NOVEL

Choucas is a work of fiction; Nałkowska describes it herself as a "novel" and gives it the subtitle *An International Novel* (*powieść internacjonalna*). It is not autobiography as such; neither is it *reportage*, nor a description of Leysin (which is not named in the text). The sanatoria town in the Swiss Alps in 1925 constitutes rather the background, the chief focus being the "foreigners" the narrator meets there. The precise genre status of the work is nevertheless unstable, difficult to define. To some extent it is indeed autobiographical, or at least appears so—"fiction posing as autobiography, or maybe the reverse" (Kirchner 2011, 235)— yet the identity and personality of the narrator remains obscure and undeveloped within the novel itself. The narrator, it is clear from the Polish grammatical endings (e.g. past tense of verbs), is a woman, but she is never named; we should therefore beware of assuming the narrator is called Zofia Nałkowska. Likewise, during the course of the opening chapter, as the couple feed the birds, it becomes clear that her companion is a man, but it is never made explicit who exactly he is: husband, lover, friend; he too is never named. In the English translation, which makes no gender distinctions for verb endings or adjectives, the gender of the protagonists is initially rendered even more obscure. Even to describe them as "protagonists" is misguided, because the real object of the narrator's attention is not their relationship but the company she meets in the villa-pension, tea rooms, hotels, or other sanatoria. According to Hanna Kirchner, the chief function of the narrator is her "role as witness"—"reporter of the events and phenomena surrounding her": "She collects this knowledge *en passant*, sharing with the patients of the 'international' pension meals, walks, entertainments. She converses, listens to confessions, contemplates the fates and mentality of the sick people. The plot is a shared, collective one, like the communal table in the pension, but at the same time opens up to new happenings, times, countries, biographies" (2011, 235).

The main focus of the novel is thus the interrelationship between the different human beings the narrator meets—as individuals, but also as representatives of their respective European nations, including the various colonies (Madame de Carfort is the wife of a French officer stationed in Morocco; Monsieur Curchaud is a plantation owner in Cambodia, then part of French Indochina). They are not one-dimensional national stereotypes, yet they betray stereotypical nation-specific sentiments and prejudices in relation to one another. As Włodzimierz Bolecki emphasizes in his analysis (2003), these prejudices have no rational or even ideological basis: they consist rather in internalized stereotypes culturally inherited and are driven by emotional factors rather than reasoned concerns, but they are sometimes reinforced by traumatic historical experience that is hard to rationalize and results in dangerous generalizations, for example, about all Germans or all Englishmen. The narrator senses danger ahead for civilized interrelations. Meanwhile, she also shows how perfectly friendly individuals, apparently reasonable and civilized, can be full of negative emotional baggage toward individual representatives of other nations, reinforcing stereotypes that encourage hatred, as in the case of affable Monsieur Verdy who hates all Germans because he lost his only son at the Battle of the Marne, or amiable Miss Norah who loathes the Irish, or the Spanish nationalist Carrizales who detests Arabs.

Hatred is underlined as a driving force behind international intercourse. And here we encounter one of the most dramatic subtexts of the novel: the Armenian exiles who witnessed the genocide of 1915–16. Interethnic hatred was a theme not unknown to contemporary Polish literature, 1924 having seen the publication of Stefan Żeromski's novel *The Coming Spring* (*Przedwiośnie*), which includes a description of the violent massacre of Armenians in Baku in 1918.[9] Specific issues relating to the Armenians will be explained in notes to the current translation.

Reflecting on this hatred, the narrator observes that what unites two nations is often their shared hatred of a third; so there will never be peace, because how can all nations unite if they have no one left to hate? "I could not resist the thought that the brotherhood of two nations consists precisely in the fact that they will unite against a third. And hence the brotherhood of all nations, all people, seems impossible. For *against whom* will they unite?" (chapter 20, Nałkowska's emphases).

Despite the narrator's lack of focus on herself, her position on these particular issues is not neutral and is often conveyed through the characters to whom she appears most sympathetic: the two Armenian women, Mademoiselle Hovsepian and "little" Sossé Papazian, and the exiled Russian Madame Wogdeman, who—we eventually learn—is not a disenfranchised Russian princess who had lost all to the Revolution (as the narrator initially assumes), but an exile out of choice, part of the Bolshevik establishment who had fled her homeland for *moral* reasons. These three characters, each in her own way, express aspects of an ideological position or, perhaps more correctly, an existential position that is not exactly pacifistic, but humanitarian, motivated by sympathy for our common humanity, yet one that is ultimately tragic and pessimistic.

Mademoiselle Hovsepian repeats several times, following discussion of some atrocity, what the narrator describes as her "naive" commentary on international relations, which becomes a kind of refrain in the novel: "one nation should not oppress another, *n'est-ce pas?*" The surface banality, however, conceals a deeper concern. The other Armenian woman, little Sossé, who is confined totally to bed, suffering apparently from both pulmonary tuberculosis and what we might describe today as a form of posttraumatic stress disorder, expresses a more nuanced position from a religious perspective that challenges traditional, nationalistic appeals to God to defend any one nation. Sossé quotes from the traditional liturgy, that of the Armenian Apostolic Church (though the narrator mentions Sossé is from a Catholic-rite family), a prayer she accepts only until the petition intrudes: "grant victory to the Christian armies. O, be Thou the refuge of the Armenian people!" (chapter 22) At this point, she rejects the prayer, claiming it contains a petition God can never grant. According to her, God should not be asked to favor any individual nation and not be invoked in any one nation's defense; she rejects such exclusivity based on the assumption that one nation is intrinsically morally superior to another. Sossé also reinforces the view of human nature as uniformly violent, irrespective of nationhood. Herself a victim of the atrocities against Armenians, she does not regard this persecution as essentially different from other violent events in world history; rather she sees it as a matter of degree, much as Nałkowska regarded war (chapter 36). War is only an extreme form of how humans treat each other anyway: just a matter of degree.

The position of Madame Wogdeman adds an important dimension: namely, the perception that ideological systems and political structures may change, but people remain essentially the same, with their complex motives, fears, and instincts intact. Hence new regimes merely end up repeating the mistakes and injustices of their predecessors: put in simple terms, power corrupts and is always exercised according to similar methods and predictable patterns of behavior. This is Wogdeman's reason for exile: the wife of a leading Bolshevik, she has witnessed at close hand how Russia's new rulers prove to be as arbitrary and cruel as the tsarist authorities they displaced—some things have remained constant: "war, imprisonments, and the power of some over the lives and deaths of others" (chapter 31).

Like the refrain of Mademoiselle Hovsepian, Wogdeman's words form another leitmotif of the novel. The sense that political change brings only a repetition of the same brutal aspects of political repression, imprisonment, and even torture had become deeply ingrained in Nałkowska's consciousness already in the early 1920s, when she witnessed former revolutionary and patriotic leaders exercising power after Poland regained independence. As the wife of Gorzechowski, a professional gendarme, she was aware of the treatment, for example, of political opponents and national minorities in the eastern borderlands. Anticipating the collection of short stories, *Walls of the World* (1931), inspired by her visits to prisoners in Grodno in the 1920s, *Choucas* already presents a similar perspective: irrespective of the ideologies of successive regimes, the mechanisms of power remain the same.

The condensed, concentrated, sometimes aphoristic style of language employed by Nałkowska in *Choucas* also finds its expression in *Walls of the World,* and reaches its most refined effectiveness in *Medallions*. These texts deploy an extremely bare, minimalistic yet evocative literary language that hinges on a perfect balance between seemingly detached objectivity (the statement of the "facts"), and the emotional and moral shock not articulated directly by the narrator but powerfully conveyed nevertheless to the reader. As with many of Nałkowska's works, not only these, one has the impression of having read a much longer text than one actually has, so dense is the compactness of expression, associations, and implications.

Toward the end of chapter 42 of *Choucas*, the narrator, on the point of departure from the sanatoria town, sums up her experience of the international community there, again emphasizing her reception of it as humanitarian and existential rather than overtly political. Her first statement may seem banal, recalling the "naive" approach of Mademoiselle Hovsepian:

> We people like to speak to one another everywhere in a different way—only our laughter and our tears mean the same across the world [...] And yet, when I resided there for several months among people speaking different languages, I always sensed that we had more in common than not in common. And what we had in common was precisely what was more important—indeed the most important. And the fact that in different locations on earth people make themselves understood through different words [...] was less important.

However, the statement is followed by something less banal: "But precisely this sufficed for things to be as they are, for there to be misunderstandings between them, hatred, war."

Although she was not religious in the sense of belonging to an established creed, Nałkowska describes the religious sentiments guiding the behavior of some of the characters, and which thus shape the broad existential canvas of the novel, including certain contemporary fashions—for example, the debates among the Christian apologist Monsieur de Flèche, the strictly traditional Catholic Madame de Carfort, the "socialist" Totsky who admires progressive contemporary theologians such as Wilfred Monod

(1867–1943) and Leonhard Ragaz (1868–1945), and the doubting seeker Sossé Papazian, so keenly attuned to suffering. While the novel gives voice to the various existential worldviews apparent in individuals of divergent nationalities and political loyalties, the narrator neither endorses nor contests the theological viewpoints underlying them. Sensitive to the human need for transcendence (which for her was expressed rather in sublime nature or in art), Nałkowska regarded religion as a crucial element in philosophical enquiry and social existence, and therefore includes it in this portrayal of human interaction.

A POLISH "MAGIC MOUNTAIN"?

The international community, the narrator's underlying concern about ideological extremes, as well as the Alpine sanatorium setting prompt comparisons with Thomas Mann's much more famous (and much longer) novel *The Magic Mountain* (*Der Zauberberg*) published in 1924.

Whether *Choucas* was influenced in some way by Mann's book is hard to establish, but it would seem, in fact, that there was no "influence" as such. The obvious similarities make it difficult to deny. Certain contemporary reviewers already made the comparison but without discussing the possibility of influence.[10] Curiously, some Polish critics have dubbed the novel the "Polish Zauberberg" even though they too have not delved beyond the mere observance of the similarity (Kraskowska 1999, 49; Bolecki 2003, 2). Yet there is no conclusive evidence that Nałkowska read *The Magic Mountain*, before or after writing *Choucas*. She does not mention it in any diary entries written between 1899 and 1939, in which she kept a detailed (though not exhaustive) record of her reading. If she did read it, she would have to have done so in the original German. Mann's novel was published in English for the first time in 1927, in French in 1931, and in Polish not until 1953.[11] She was fluent in French and Russian, but her knowledge of German was weak, at least at that time (i.e., before the German Occupation of 1939–1945).[12] Even if she did attempt to read it in German, there would not have been much time to do so between the novel's publication in November 1924 and Nałkowska's arrival in Leysin in February 1925. Her own novel began to appear already in August 1926. Seen from this perspective, it would seem that the convergence of setting and theme was coincidental—she just happened to be in a similar environment, met people there from various European countries and their colonies, and chose to write about them.

On the other hand, she must have known of *Der Zauberberg*'s existence: it was reviewed or mentioned quickly in Polish newspapers and journals with which she was certainly familiar, e.g., in the literary newspaper *Wiadomości Literackie* in April 1925.[13] Mann was popular among Polish contemporary writers: "German novelists of the Weimar Republic were widely read, especially Thomas Mann" (Miłosz 1983, 421), so the lack of any mention by Nałkowska is puzzling. Indeed, in the four volumes of her diary covering 1899–1939, she mentions only one title by Thomas Mann: *Tonio Kröger*, which she records on 30 March 1916 as having read (1976, 425). She seems unimpressed on that occasion, however, entering only one word beside the title: "uninteresting" ("*nieciekawe*"). She must have read it in German: *Tonio Kröger* was not translated into French until 1929 (by Geneviève Maury) and not into Polish until 1931 (by Leopold Staff).[14]

The lack of mention is additionally strange since Nałkowska met Mann when he visited Poland in March 1927 at the invitation of the Polish PEN Club, of which Nałkowska was a prominent member. She describes aspects of his visit in her diary (1980b, 232–36) but does not mention *The Magic Mountain*, or compare it to her own *Choucas*. On 14 March she mentions that they had "a few conversations, from which I had the impression we understood one another perfectly—though perhaps this was only one-sided" (232) without recording what they spoke about.

Furthermore, she wrote a short critical essay on Mann's novella *Ein Glück* (*Szczęście*) as part of the special feature marking his visit published in *Wiadomości Literackie* on 13 March (Nałkowska 1927b, 3). On this occasion it is clear she read Mann in Polish, as the quotations she inserts from the novella are taken word for word from Staff's translation (Mann 1924, 83–101).[15]

In a much later diary entry for October 1944, she records how she had been reading the *Confessions* of Saint Augustine, specifically mentioning the section on time and remarking how Augustine "anticipates this theme in Proust and Mann" (1996, 630); no mention is made of any specific work. Time, however, is a major concern in *The Magic Mountain,* indicating perhaps that by this stage at least, she had read it (assuming she meant here Thomas and not Heinrich). Is it possible Nałkowska resisted comparison with Mann and therefore never mentioned his novel? Maybe she thought such comparison might belittle her own work?

It is worth reflecting for a moment on Nałkowska's interpretation of *Ein Glück,* because it is symptomatic. Whereas she does not record much about Mann in her diary and appears dismissive of *Tonio Kröger,* she gives this one (early and relatively under-discussed) novella an exceptionally positive gloss. Why? First, because she sees Mann as unusually sensitive for a male writer to the female protagonist's perspective and, second, because he portrays a powerful syndrome in female emotional and erotic life that typifies many of her own protagonists. This is so not only in *Choucas* (1927)—in the behaviors of Madame Saint-Albert and Mademoiselle Alice (see below)—but also in many earlier and later novels: in *Women* (1907) or *Snakes and Roses* (1913), as well as in *Bad Love* (1928), *Boundaries* (1935), and *The Impatient Ones* (1939). Women with strong emotions or erotic feelings suffer in love (i.e., in their sexual relationships with men) because they long for exclusivity and take love too seriously. They observe how their husbands or lovers flirt with other women and thus constantly betray them; yet they are unable to behave similarly. They look on in pain, suffer in their jealousy, but have to constantly strive to appear happy (and hence attractive)—and are thereby deprived of vital energy that might be better spent on pursuing other objectives in life.

An earlier biographer and critic, Włodzimierz Wójcik, sees in *Choucas* the influence of French writers with whom Nałkowska was familiar:

> If we set aside Mann, since the author of *The Magic Mountain* mainly analyses Europe before the outbreak of the [First World] war and—according to the correct observations of Aleksander Rogalski—"as an artistic interpreter and re-creator of the life of the age, he proved to be strangely insensitive to the fundamental spiritual or intellectual characteristics of the inter-war age," then we can recognize Nałkowska's real literary inspirations as being Barbusse and Duhamel, and possibly also Dorgelès. (Wójcik 1973, 180; Rogalski 1963, 359)

Specific titles mentioned by Wójcik are Henri Barbusse's *Under Fire* (*Le Feu,* 1916); Georges Duhamel's *Lives of the Martyrs* (*Vie des martyrs,* 1917) and *Civilization* (1918); and *Wooden Crosses* (*Les Croix de bois,* 1919) by Roland Dorgelès (1973, 180). There are indeed several references to Duhamel and to Barbusse in Nałkowska's diary during this period: to her reading of Barbusse's *Under Fire, Clarté* (1919) and *Hell* (*L'Enfer,* 1908) (1980b, 65), to reading Duhamel (1980, 290; see also 292–94: Duhamel visited Poland in October 1926). Dorgelès is not specifically listed by Nałkowska. A quotation from Duhamel's *Entretiens dans le tumult: chronique contemporaine 1918–1919* (1919) is included in the text of *Choucas* (end of chapter 31).

What then does *Choucas* have in common with Mann's novel, and how does it differ? Mann's book was set in Davos, in a German-speaking region in the eastern part of Switzerland; Nałkowska's is set in a French-speaking environment near Lake

Geneva. The historical period is also different: Mann's work deals with European society before the First World War and ends with the main protagonist's participation in the war, one of countless numbers who perished on its battlefields. Nałkowska's reflects society after the war, in the mid-1920s, when various extreme ideologies were gathering momentum both at home in Poland and in Europe. Her novel not only reflects on the barbarism and losses of the First World War (the story of Monsieur Verdy's son) and the genocide against Armenians. It also illustrates other catastrophic developments: the story of Est, the Jewish student from Bucharest and his experience of antisemitism; the abuses of Soviet power witnessed by Madame Wogdeman; the struggles of various colonies in North Africa and the Far East against their imperial masters, and the suppression of liberation movements with violence. On the other hand, Nałkowska's narrator seems to focus much more on the national and cultural elements that divide people rather than on the philosophical or ideological. There are no fundamental conflicts on the scale of that between Naphta and Settembrini, or between their intellectual approach to life and the Dionysian attitude embodied in Mynheer Peeperkorn.

Finding herself in a similar environment to the fictional Hans Castorp in Davos, similarly exposed to a cross-section of representatives of the European nations—mostly privileged people with a somewhat superior attitude to those down below, it is not surprising that Nałkowska's narrator also speaks about the things that impressed the writer the most, namely people's attitudes toward each other, as well as aspects of their daily routine: the cure, mealtimes, walks in the mountains, the magnificent scenery, the political debates of the day. The society the narrator describes, however, does not include only people suffering from tuberculosis. Monsieur Curchaud has come to enjoy the winter sports, as have the English couple Mr and Mrs Vigil. Others are refugees housed in the sanatoria hotels and pensions by the Red Cross, namely the three Armenians. The Russians, Madame Wogdeman and Mademoiselle Alice, also refugees, similarly have nowhere else to go. Others are indeed patients suffering from either bone (Miss Norah) or lung (Est, Verdy, Fuchs) tuberculosis; Madame de Carfort is likewise on a cure but we are not told anything other than that the climate in Morocco is harmful to her condition.

Unlike Mann, Nałkowska's narrator is not interested in the strictly medical aspects, and the fascinating history of Leysin and its pioneering doctors are mentioned only in passing. The description of Norah lying naked on her balcony exposed to the healing rays of the sun is an exception. There is no figure comparable to Mann's Hofrat Behrens; no detailed descriptions of medical examinations, of how X-rays work (a new technology in those days), or of how lung operations are performed. However, like Mann, she also draws a parallel between bodily sickness and moral sickness, and the sickness of ideological extremes.

Choucas is not about sickness as such, however. In both novels, discussions of political and philosophical differences may take place with impunity in the rarefied environment above the clouds, but when they are put into practice down in the real world—the colonializing imperialism, for example, of Madame de Carfort or Carrezales or Curchaud—the violence meted out to their opponents, to those less powerful than the perpetrators, can be catastrophic. At the same time, however, despite her tolerant and progressive spirit, Nałkowska's narrator is not entirely free of colonial attitudes: albeit in a positive manner, she uses such vocabulary as "oriental" (Madame de Carfort's beauty) or "exotic" (Mademoiselle Hovsepian) to describe human Others, i.e., people not from the mainstream cultures of contemporary Europe (among which she appears to include herself as a Pole—though she is sensitive to the fact that only Monsieur Verdy expresses any interest in Poland); as a colonial, Madame de Carfort is portrayed as more stereotypically French than the French.

Meanwhile the rarefied moral climate is paralleled by the rarefied air: at such high altitude—looking down on the world from privileged heights, removed from "normal" social inter-course—regular responsibilities no longer seem to apply. During the Carnival party held in the villa-pension (chapter 18), which recalls many precise details of the Carnival scene in *The Magic Mountain* (the portrayal of this event is strikingly similar—although being resident at the same time of year, it would not have been unexpected that she would attend a similar party as Hans Castorp), Nałkowska's narrator speaks of how the guests and patients seem like a group of lost children for whom no one is responsible:

> I imagined they were all like children. Unprotected and exposed to every danger. So alone, thrown back on their own resources in this alien mountain house amid the snows. Who was to keep watch over them? [...] healthy and sick, young and old—a collec-tion of thoughtless children confronted by the seriousness of life for whom no one was responsible.

NOVEL VERSUS DIARY

While in Leysin, Nałkowska recorded in her diary her observa-tions of the actual place and the people whom she encountered, as well as aspects of her own internal life—many elements of which also find their way into the novel (1980b, 153–70). At the time of Nałkowska's stay (early February to mid-April 1925), Leysin was a well-known resort, second only in Switzerland to Davos.[16]

The novel, as already mentioned, does not refer to Leysin by name, while the narrator seems more interested in the topog-raphy and the beauties of nature than in the medical cures, and stands as an independent text in its own right, separate from the literal, physical place that inspired it. However, the diary illumi-nates particular inspirations and is even the source of precise phrases and descriptions directly transposed into the novel's text. For example, many exact details appear both in Nałkowska's novel and in her diary: the cog (or rack and pinion) train, the viaduct, the steep tunnel inside the rocks, the top station with its walkway over a bridge into the second floor of the hotel, the Grand Hôtel itself, the heliotherapy treatment undertaken in the novel by Miss Norah, the *repos complet* (mentioned in chapter 21 of the novel), a two-hour period of daily rest and total silence recommended by the doctors and enforced by the local police. Also in the diary are the prototypes for many of the novel's characters.

The correspondences and discrepancies between the diary record (which, as also mentioned above, was not generally available to readers or researchers until 1980) and the novel also reveal Nałkowska's writing technique: she recorded what she observed as she went along in order to return to it later and exploit the material for fictional-artistic purposes when she had more time and found herself in surroundings more conducive to creative writing. The diary could be said to fulfil several functions at once: it was a record of witnessed people, places, and events (which to some extent we may regard as objective, or "true," albeit selective); a repository of material gathered for future artistic exploitation—what Hanna Kirchner calls a "literary larder" (2011, 799); a "literary" reworking of the writer's experience (Nałkowska said of herself that she perceived everything "in a literary way"); and a means of actually "writing herself," i.e., a medium through which she processed material and reflections that went into her own self-creation.

The modest pension or small sanatorium, usually described as a "villa" (in the contemporary context, this implied a modern building constructed from stone, as opposed to a traditional wooden chalet), is also not named in the novel. The anonymity, however, is not maintained for long, since the location can easily be established on the basis of the configuration of mountains and valleys visible from the villa's balconies: the position of the Dents du Midi, the Chamossaire, the valleys of the Rhône and Grande Eau. We know from the diary (1980b, 154) that the villa-pension was called "Pension de la Forêt." Its position can be roughly located from that very configuration of mountains, although Nałkowska does not give the address, except its being in Leysin-Feydey (the top part of the village, where the large sanatoria were built from the 1890s). It appears the pension soon changed its name, because it does not appear in subsequent lists of sanatoria, hotels, and pensions in Leysin.[17] It has been possible, however, to identify the building once housed by "Pension de la Forêt" as the one now consisting of private flats called "La Coccinelle" on Avenue Sécretan, the road that leads horizontally west across the mountainside from the station at Leysin-Feydey, a position that also coincides with incidents in the novel: it is clear from the novel's closing scene, for example, that the departing train can be observed from windows and balconies of the pension.

The trains appearing in the novel are described in the diary and still run on the same routes today. For example, the grumpy, morose "personality" of the cog train (chapter 15), recorded in the diary entry for 12 February 1925, appears as follows: "From Aigle we were carried up the mountain by the little electric cog train, groaning softly from exertion and dissatisfaction" (1980b, 156). Aigle is not mentioned by name in the novel. In the diary entry for 4 April, she describes a five-kilometre walk down from Leysin to neighbouring Le Sépey, where she and her companions board a different train: the narrow-gauge, single-track electric train that takes them up to Les Diablerets through magnificent scenery along cliff ledges and over narrow bridges above dramatic chasms, and then back down to Aigle and the flat Rhône Valley (1980b, 162–164). Again, in the novel, she does not mention by name the precise geographical locations, but elements of this journey are transcribed into chapter 25, sometimes in precise detail or even word for word, such as the description of the local peasant women in their black hats and dresses spreading manure over the fields (1980b, 163). Other descriptions of the mountains, the local natural world, the tentative coming of spring, various hikes, and other expeditions are similarly transcribed from the diary into the text of the novel.

Sometimes, Nałkowska exploits details she has recorded but gives the place another name: for example, on 15 February, she describes the hotel where they spent the first few days of their stay, calling it the Hotel "de la Gare," with its fiery Spanish proprietess who loved to dance to a relentless pianola ("in the morning in her dressing-gown, in the afternoon in a jumper, and in the evening in a revealing, low-cut, brightly coloured dress,"), Italian waitress with gold headband and gold earrings, and husband who played billiards and accompanied his wife's singing on the mandolin (1980b, 157–58)—all details precisely transcribed into chapter 17 of the novel, where the hotel is renamed Toscana. Her most evocative descriptions of interiors are reserved, however, for the Palace Hotel and its *Jardin d'hiver* (chapter 15). This location is mentioned in the diary only in passing, as the venue for the charity bazaar (described in chapter 23), and as "the most beautiful hotel in the vicinity" (1980b, 160). However, the hotel appears in detail in the novel itself, and a visit to the location identifies beyond doubt that the inspiration was the Grand Hôtel now owned by the Leysin American School, and recently renovated as "La Belle Époque" campus. All the details described by Nałkowska's narrator conform to the actual building—from the fact that the hotel is "invisible" from below, hidden by forest and rocks, to the footbridge that connects the uppermost station of the cog railway to the second floor, to the stained-glass cupola in the ceiling of the conservatory.

The diary also mentions individuals who were clearly prototypes for characters in the novel, although here Nałkowska changes their names as well as other specific details: the beautiful wife of a French officer resident in Morocco (1980b, 165–66); a Spanish gentleman who supports not only Alfonso XIII and the military dictator Miguel Primo de Rivera, but their colonial policy in North Africa (165); the group of Armenian exiles, witnesses to the genocide (158, 168); the Romanian student who is a victim of antisemitism (167). Under altered names, their personalities, opinions, and prejudices are reworked into the novel's text. Nałkowska also mentions in these diary passages what appear to be the same books discussed by characters in the novel, and they are therefore a useful source of background information, as no Polish edition of the novel to date identifies them. These are explained in notes to the text of the translation.

What is especially interesting, however, is that Nałkowska puts into the mouths of entirely fictional, invented figures—or rather, figures for whom she provides no "real-life" models in the diary—additional passages from the diary that relate to herself. She transposes even exact sentences, where she expresses her own fears, for example about ageing, from the diary into the novel, putting them into the mouth of the fictional Madame Saint-Albert. This raises a question as to the purpose of this character in the novel, as does the presence of other female characters, notably Mademoiselle Alice and Madame Wogdeman, for whom no obvious models likewise appear in the diary (no post-1917 Russian exiles are mentioned in the diary—only the model for Monsieur Totsky, who, like the fictional Totsky, is not an exile in the same sense as Wogdeman, being described rather as a Swiss citizen of Russian origin). One should beware of claiming that these fictional female characters are to some extent the *portes paroles* of the narrator, and also of the author herself, but I do suggest it as a possibility.

In the diary entry for 13 March 1925, we read the following confessions, which coincide almost word for word with sentiments expressed in chapters 15 and 27 by Madame Saint-Albert:

> Earlier in life I flattered myself that I would know how to grow old. And yet I have experienced this very crisis with great dif-

ficulty, deeply and precisely. I look at everything around me, at everything current in life, as though it were something that has come after me. I don't look at life, *I look back at it.* And this is not some serene form of melancholy. These are attacks of despair, which can only be silenced or suppressed by the thought that there is a way out: that I will die. (1980b, 160; Nałkowska's emphases)

The narrator of the diary has not yet reached, unlike Madame Saint-Albert, a point of no return: she is still moved by the beauties of nature, still reads and enjoys a vast number of books, and still knows how to keep up outward appearances. Yet, the knowledge of her ageing weighs heavily on her perception of herself, her vanity and growing sense of worthlessness. The words contained here are repeated more or less verbatim in the novel by Madame Saint-Albert (chapter 27):

I am simply ashamed to be old. My eternal aesthetic approach to myself is bankrupt.—I talk more and more about other people, think about other people—in order to deflect my own attention away from myself. How ashamed I am of the fact I'm no longer slim and especially that ultimately it's all one and the same, what I'm like. But—I repeat—outward appearances are maintained, I am, as though nothing had happened [...]. And despite enjoying and flaunting my youth since I was fifteen years old, it is only now that I realize that youth is a trump card. Youth is not a state of being, it's a value, an addendum to everything else. And old age is the taking away of value from everything. (1980b, 160–61)

The role of Mademoiselle Alice in the novel and what she may represent or convey is not so obvious or explicit, nor is its connection with Nałkowska. In the novel, Nałkowska's narrator attempts to explain the particular crisis experienced by the twenty-two-year-old Alice. Young and attractive and emanating a strong sexual charge, Alice is driven by personal vanity and also by her innate and entirely natural sexual instincts to actively seek the attention of men. At one and the same time, however, she feels a compulsion to resist their demands once their desire has been seriously aroused in order to claim—irrespective of her own behavior—that they do not respect her, thereby eventually rejecting and attempting to shame and humiliate them. Alice attracts the narrator's interest, not because her dramas are important in themselves, but because she perccives Alice as exemplifying a particular syndrome in culturally determined, womanly behavior: "a specific pattern of constantly shifting equilibrium between defeat and victory. Her need to arouse passion in men was just as strong and irrevocable as her need to triumph over it" (chapter 16).

Torn perpetually between her need to flirt, to assert her sexuality and attract admirers, and to triumph over them by keeping intact her virginity and self-respect like some inviolable fortress, Alice is shown to truly suffer existentially. When she falls in love seriously and unrequitedly, this time with Monsieur de Flèche, she is unable to control her instincts or conceal them from him or from other people. Is the narrator (and her author) making some statement here about female sexuality and the contemporary perceptions of it—even recalling perhaps the young Nałkowska's demand (at the 1907 Polish Women's Congress) for the rejection of the double standard, for women's sexual equality with men and what she called at that time their right to "the whole of life"? On the one hand, Alice is an innocent, a natural—she possesses no stereotypical feminine wiles and is unashamedly candid in her confessions, since her intention is not to harm others, only to satisfy her egocentric need for "danger" and "anguish." On the other hand, her suffering could be perceived as the consequence of her lack of education and self-understanding, which leave her unable to manage the power of her own feelings, or quite simply: biology. On several occasions in the novel, she is compared to spring—a passionate and natural being, whose instinctive reactions are an affront to the majority of society. The narrator passes no judgement, merely lends a sympathetic ear to her confidences. Nałkowska remained locked in her Modernist conviction of the ultimate incompatibility of the sexes and of the role of biology in determining fatal attraction, especially in women. However, the human experiences portrayed in the novel, both intimate and collective, are not so much—or not only—autobiographical or exclusive to women, as reflective of Nałkowska's pessimism concerning human interrelationship in general.

NOTES

1. The first volume of the diaries to appear, censored in communist Poland, was entitled *Wartime Diaries* (*Dzienniki czasu wojny,* 1970), republished in 1996 as volume 5 (1939–1944) of the complete set with the excised parts restored. The other volumes are: 1: 1899–1905 (published 1975); 2: 1909–1917 (1976); 3: 1918–1929 (1980); 4: 1930–1939 (1988); 6: Part 1, 1945–1948, Part 2, 1949–1952, Part 3, 1953–1954 (2000). All volumes are edited and annotated by Hanna Kirchner and published by the Warsaw publisher Czytelnik. Apart from Kirchner's recent chapter "Dzieło nieznane" (2011, 789–826), the following critical works may be of interest: Marszałek 2003; Fołtyniak 2004; Fitas 2011.

2. Here there is no space to provide a complete survey of her literary output. Readers of Polish are referred to the recent biography by Hanna Kirchner, which also contains analytical chapters on her literary works, *Nałkowska albo życie pisane* (Warsaw: Wydawnictwo W.A.B., 2011). Introductory surveys may be found (in English) by Kirchner (1999) and Borkowska (2001a, 255–321; and 2001b, 150–55), and (in Polish) in Ewa Kraskowska (1999, 38–74). See also my brief critical review of her pre-1939 works "Politics and Ethics of Human Relations" in *A History of Polish Literature and Culture: New Perspectives on the Twentieth and Twenty-first Centuries,* edited by Przemysław Czapliński, Joanna Niżyńska and Tamara Trojanowska [forthcoming]. The only critical assessments specifically of *Choucas* of which I am aware, apart from the contemporary 1927 reviews,

are the chapter in Kirchner's book "Cudzoziemskie ptaki" (2011, 235–46), the chapter in an earlier biography (Wójcik 1973, 170–208), and the article by Włodzimierz Bolecki (2003).

3. *My Animals* (*Moje zwierzęta*, 1915), *Book about My Friends* (*Księga o przyjaciołach*, 1927), and *Among Animals* (*Między zwierzętami*, 1934).

4. Zofia Nałkowska (2000) *Medallions*, translated by Diana Kuprel. Evanston, IL: Northwestern University Press.

5. All translations from Nałkowska's diaries are my own—U.P.

6. A list of the reviews is provided in *Słownik współczesnych pisarzy polskich* (Warsaw: Państwowe Wydawnictwo Naukowe, Volume 2: 534, 1964). The reviews are discussed by Wójcik (1973, 176–77) and Kirchner (2011, 239).

7. See, for example: *Handbook of the Birds of Europe, the Middle East and North Africa: The Birds of the Western Palearctic*. Volume 8: *Crows to Finches* (Oxford: Oxford University Press, 1994); and *Crows and Jays: A Guide to the Crows, Jays and Magpies of the World*, edited by Steve Madge and Hilary Burn (London: Croom Helm, 1994). I am grateful to Erika and Nick Panagakis for identifying the English name of the bird in question as the Alpine chough.

8. I am likewise indebted to Swiss ornithologist Jérôme Fournier for providing this extra information which explains why Nałkowska used the name *choucas* and clears up the confusion over whether they are jackdaws, and for taking me to see the birds in their summer habitat in the mountains above Leysin.

9. Stefan Żeromski (2007), *The Coming Spring*, translated by Bill Johnston (Budapest: Central European University Press).

10. See the untitled review undersigned by A. Stawar in the journal *Dźwignia* no. 2–3 (1927): 55–57.

11. English translation by H.T. Lowe-Porter (London: Secker and Warburg, 1927); French by Maurice Betz (Paris: Fayard, 1931). The Polish version was published in two volumes in 1953, volume 1 translated by Józef Kramsztyk, volume 2 by Jan Łukowski (pseudonym of the philosopher Władysław Tartarkiewicz).

12. I am most grateful to Professor Hanna Kirchner for our discussions on this topic on 24 April 2012 and again on 30 March 2013. Professor Kirchner sees no influence of *The Magic Mountain* on *Choucas*.

13. Review entitled "Nowa powieść Tomasza Manna 'Der Zauberberg'" undersigned by "jk" in *Wiadomości Literackie*, no. 15 (1925): 1.

14. She records having read a few early works by Mann's brother, Heinrich Mann (1871–1950), to which she seems to have been more positively inclined, including *Diana* (one of the three parts of *Die Göttinnen oder Die drei Romane der Herzogin von Assy*, 1903, translated into Polish in 1930), recorded as read on 21 August 1912 (1976, 235); *Źli* (*Die Bösen*, 1908), recorded as read on 17 January 1916 (1976, 422); and *Cudowne* (*Das Wunderbare. Novellen*, 1897), recorded as read on 29 September 1916 (1976, 463). Although she records the titles in Polish, it seems she read them in German.

15. The 1924 collection of Staff's translations of Mann includes six stories, although it is entitled only *Tristan* (Mann, 1924). Nałkowska's essay was republished in the volume *Widzenia bliskie i dalekie* (Nałkowska 1957, 110–12).

16. I am most grateful to local historian Véronique Bernard for providing me with materials on Leysin at the time of Nałkowska's stay. For a detailed picture of Leysin's history as a sanatoria village, see her bilingual dvd film: *Leysin, 100 ans d'histoire 1860–1960/ Leysin, 100 Years of History*: a production by Véronique Bernard and Pierre-Alain Frey (2008). It was from an old photograph shown in this film of the Pension de la Fôret (the name is inscribed on a side wall)—a former clinic for child patients, subsequently a boardinghouse, and now a block of private flats that was long ago renamed—that I was able to identify the building where Nałkowska stayed in 1925. On the history of Leysin, see also Liliane Desponds, *Histoire et reconversion d'une ville à la montagne* (Yens-sur-Morges: Editions Cabédita, 1993).

17. It is not listed, for example, in *Leysin, station medicale. Témoignages recuellis par Maurice André* (Le Mont-sur-Lausanne: Editions Les Iles futures, 2d ed., 2007).

BIBLIOGRAPHY

Bolecki, Włodzimierz. 2003. "Ludobójstwo i początki prozy nowoczesnej (*Choucas* Zofii Nałkowskiej)." *Arkusz* 5: 31–49.

Borkowska, Grażyna. 2001a. *Alienated Women: A Study on Polish Women's Fiction 1845–1918*, translated by Ursula Phillips. Budapest: Central European University Press.

———. 2001b. "The Feminization of Culture: Polish Women's Literature, 1900–1945." In *A History of Central European Women's Writing*, edited by Celia Hawkesworth, 150–64. Basingstoke: Palgrave Macmillan.

Fitas, Adam. 2011. *Zamiast eposu. Rzecz o Dziennikach Zofii Nałkowskiej.* Lublin: Wydawnictwo Katolickiego Uniwersytetu Lubelskiego.

Fołtyniak, Anna. 2004. *Między "pisać Nałkowską" a Nałkowskiej "czytaniem siebie." Narracyjna tożsamość podmiotu w "Dziennikach."* Kraków: Universitas.

Kirchner, Hanna. 1984. "Nałkowska—prolegomena do Gombrowicza." In *Gombrowicz i krytycy,* edited by Zdzisław Łapiński, 573–86. Kraków: Wydawnictwo Literackie.

———. 1999. "Zofia Nałkowska." In *Dictionary of Literary Biography,* Volume 215: *Twentieth-Century Eastern European Writers,* First Series, edited by Steven Serafin, 273–82. Detroit: Gale Research Company.

———. 2011. *Nałkowska albo życie pisane.* Warsaw: Wydawnictwo W.A.B.

Kraskowska, Ewa. 1999. *Piórem niewieścim. Z problemów prozy kobiecej dwudziestolecia międzywojennego.* Poznań: Wydawnictwo Naukowe Uniwersytetu im. Adama Mickiewicza.

Mann, Tomasz. 1924. *Tristan,* translated [from German into Polish] by Leopold Staff, 83–101. Warsaw: Nakładem B. Rudzkiego.

Marszałek, Magdalena. 2003. *"Życie i papier." Autobiograficzny projekt Zofii Nałkowskiej "Dzienniki" 1899–1954.* Kraków: Universitas.

Miłosz, Czesław. 1993. *The History of Polish Literature.* 2d ed. Berkeley: University of California Press.

Nałkowska, Zofia. 1927a. *Choucas. Powieść internacjonalna.* Warsaw: Gebethner i Wolff.

———. 1927b. "Szczęście." *Wiadomości literackie* 11: 3.

———. 1938. *Choucas. Powieść internacjonalna*. 2d ed. Lwów and Warsaw: Książnica-Atlas.

———. 1957. "Szczęście." In *Widzenia bliskie i dalekie*, edited by Tadeusz Breza, Bogusław Kuczyński, Wilhelm Mach, and Jerzy Zawiejski, 110–12. Warsaw: Czytelnik.

———. 1960. *Choucas. Powieść internacjonalna*. Warsaw: Czytelnik.

———. 1975. *Dzienniki*. Volume 1: 1899–1905, edited and introduced by Hanna Kirchner. Warsaw: Czytelnik.

———. 1976. *Dzienniki*. Volume 2: 1909–1917, edited and introduced by Hanna Kirchner. Warsaw: Czytelnik.

———. 1980a. *Choucas. Powieść internacjonalna*. Warsaw: Czytelnik.

———. 1980b. *Dzienniki*. Volume 3: 1918–1929, edited and introduced by Hanna Kirchner. Warsaw: Czytelnik.

———. 1988. *Dzienniki*. Volume 4, Part 2: 1935–1939, edited and introduced by Hanna Kirchner. Warsaw: Czytelnik.

———. 1996. *Dzienniki*. Volume 5: 1939–1944, edited and introduced by Hanna Kirchner. Warsaw: Czytelnik.

———. 2000. *Medallions*, translated by Diana Kuprel. Evanston, IL: Northwestern University Press.

Rogalski, Aleksander. 1963. *Most nad przepaścią. O Tomaszu Mannie*. Warsaw: Instytut Wydawniczy PAX.

Wójcik, Włodzimierz. 1973. *Zofia Nałkowska*. Warsaw: Wiedza Powszechna.

CHOUCAS

1

"Make the pieces a bit smaller today, I implore you," I gently protest.

Silence.

"No, the ones I'm making are quite small enough."

"All right. But don't you see? They often fly off with pieces like that when they can't swallow them."

"No. They're just trying the taste, making up their minds."

Now I'm simply lost for words.

"Making up their minds," I repeat bitterly and say no more.

Things take their usual course.

Tiny slices of white bread sprinkled with sugar lie soaking in warm milk.

Once the bread has absorbed enough taste, we scrape the snow off the balcony balustrade and arrange the pieces carefully with a teaspoon—and then wait for the choucas to come or awaken.

Perhaps they'll fly in from the deep, dark blue valleys or return from the white, even higher mountains. Some mornings there's no sign of them before nine or later. Other times they arrive too soon, before anything's ready.

I suggest I arrange the bread myself—only on one side of the balustrade so the choucas have somewhere to sit comfortably, won't trample on the food with their feet or knock it to the ground.

"No, that won't be necessary. I know how they like it."

Precisely. There's always an answer to whatever I suggest, heaps of arguments. And there's nothing I can do.

Steaming with milk, the bread lies on the balustrade in the clear frosty air. Instead of cold, the fierce, piercing, joyous heat of the sun streams into our room through the open doors of the balcony.

But there are no choucas. The day's most important business has not yet begun.

Sparrows, the same the world over, arrive instead—maybe a little smaller than the ones in the valley[1] but just as bold and spirited, rarely standing on ceremony.

There are not many. They appear as if not from the air, but from out of the walls, from beneath the balustrade or awning, even from under the floor. ·

We prepare separate food for them. Crumbs usually—without milk and sugar, scattered directly on the floor.

It's an odd thing, but the sparrows seem to know this. They hardly ever hop onto the balustrade and eat only what's meant for them. Eat unconcernedly, taking their time, poking about in the crumbs with their beaks and breaking down every crumb into tiny grains, which they peck up to the last morsel. A sparrow will peck once, wag its tail three times and then watch intently with one or other of its little black eyes.

They are not afraid of anything; leap up, linger on the ground, dash about, flitting between the legs of the cane chairs like grey mice, constantly repeating their "*che, che.*"

We have no idea what they're trying to say. But if Mademoiselle Hovsepian, who lives underneath us, says "*che, che,*" then we know she means: no.[2]

Three unusual things happened with these sparrows.

One sparrow, for no apparent reason, suddenly lost consciousness and fell to the ground with its claws outstretched. We immediately rushed to its aid.[3] Carried inside and nourished with

4

warm milk, it cleared its throat, opened its black eyes and then flew off from my open hand straight out of the window, as if no explanation were required.

Another—likewise for no apparent reason—dropped from the food-stacked balcony into our room, sat on the edge of the desk and then, once it had examined both of us carefully, returned to where it had come from quite unperturbed.

A third landed from somewhere else, from a place known only to itself, while we—he and I—were sitting on the balcony, and perched on the armrest of my chair holding something white in its beak.

I thought it was a piece of bread, but it was crumpled white tissue.

The sparrow tarried a little between us with the white object in its beak but then abandoned us leaving only surprise and a feeling of distaste.

Certainly, close proximity to animals can create puzzling and disturbing situations, just as it can with people. But who is able to forgo the joys of co-existence because of that?

2

"Have they come yet?" I direct my question towards the balcony from inside the room.

"No, there's no sign of them."

A small cloud floats across the middle of the blue sky, beneath the sun. It attaches itself for a moment to the summit of the Chamossaire on the other side of the valley, splits into little feathery shreds and tassels, then breaks away and moves on.

But we can no longer see the delightful, smooth valley of the Rhône spread out in the depths to the right, enclosed by the towering peaks of the Dents du Midi white with snow. Flat cloud fills the valley like a sea of flour dust, its white powdery substance drifting gently upwards. It is already spreading, pouring into the narrower, precipitous crosswise gorge of the Grande Eau lying directly beneath us. Our balcony and balustrade seem as though poised over the very edge of the sea, which is drenched in sunlight, dazzlingly white. Another moment—and we no longer see anything in the white obscurity that blocks the gaping mouth of the balcony.

"Exactly as if someone had hung up an eiderdown," I hear the begrudging remark.

Now it's possible to plunge our naked arms into the "eiderdown," catch the snow as it begins to fall—ah, how it falls!—onto the balustrade with the waiting bread, onto our faces, knees, the chintz cushions on the cane chairs.

One could sit for hours like this staring at the strange vertically hanging sea, sweeping one's eyes over the flying snow.

And then the whole balcony with its balustrade and orange-and-white striped awning, our whole villa even, begins to sail gently upward without a jolt, at an oblique angle, in the opposite direction to the falling snow.

Suddenly a muffled shriek: "The choucas are here!"

We lie flat on our reclining chairs, pretending not to be there.[4]

Finally they appear out of the white obscurity of the air.

One bird moves sideways across the open mouth of the balcony, almost motionless as though drawn on a thread. Another flashes across a corner of the opening, displaying its black belly and red feet tucked underneath like little twigs of coral. Yet another circles directly over the balustrade where we've laid out the bread, flapping its wings and not knowing where to set down those coral feet.

"He says he 'knows how they like it'," I think to myself with irony.

Others glide, hover, or sail past slowly in a whole flock. In the open mouth of the balcony they look like fish drifting beyond the bare wall of an aquarium.

One bird settled at last on the balustrade—wary, timid, dignified. Bending forward, it pecks with its yellow bill at the soft pieces of bread and swallows one of them. Black, sleek, glistening, with a gentle head and benign look in its round eye, more like a black pigeon than a member of the crow family—but more shapely with longer, black-and-red legs.

But it took a piece so large it couldn't be swallowed at once (because it was true the pieces weren't small enough) and flew away—not directly upward like other birds, but downwards, as if falling involuntarily, helplessly into the dizzying chasm of the valley.

Two new ones take its place. One sits sideways, perfectly visible, trusting, scarcely a couple of feet from our eyes. It pecks in an abstemious, somewhat studied manner, perhaps indeed "trying the taste." The other, more timid and barely clinging to the balustrade with its red claw, beats its wings, grabs two or three pieces of bread, then tears away plunging into the abyss in a gesture of despair.

Another five birds appear at once: feed, cling to the balustrade, and fall away. Suddenly there are eight of them; a moment later only two: their exquisite yellow bills—the color of straw, rather long but beautifully shaped and strangely gentle—sweep up every morsel of tasty bread. But no matter. We never spread all the food on the balustrade in one go. A second portion stands ready in a cup on the washstand.[5]

Choucas do not caw like jackdaws, rather they warble or shrill delicately, like the chirruping of our own swallows and swifts.[6] And they are very peaceable. I never saw them fight with their yellow bills among themselves, even when several descended on the balcony at the same time and couldn't all reach the food.

It can happen however that a choucas becomes angry. Then it behaves very strangely. It lifts its right leg—always the right leg!—and strikes, or rather kicks, another choucas standing in its way. It does it swiftly, in a way quite unexpected, yet decisive.

And the other bird doesn't even have time to contemplate revenge since it loses its balance immediately and tumbles, flapping its wings helplessly, into white nothingness.

7

3

But a day passes or maybe only an hour—and suddenly the white obscurity is no longer there beyond the windows.

It has stopped snowing, the curtain of mist fallen away without trace. The wild blazing mountain sun, full of the finest healing virtues, advances across the blue sky, as eyes are entranced by the far distances, intense whiteness, bright light of bleached summits, fluffy white forests and contours of valleys softened by snow.

A joyful young voice rings out from a distant balcony on the same floor:

"Thien dobhy panu! Jaka pienkna pogoda!"[7]

Thus Miss Norah Tharp, our villa's most cheerful resident, calls in Polish.

A shouted conversation begins. In English now, Miss Norah asks if we are going for a walk.

Naturally, we're going for a walk. Everyone is going for a walk. Heavy snow has fallen—so once again there'll be skiing, bobsleigh and small luge racing.

Clusters of high-spirited folk can be seen zigzagging across the slopes, clad in white or multicolored woolens, brown and red sheepskins. Children are dressed entirely in white, except for their red woolly hats, and women in tricot tunics and patterned knickerbockers, thick stockings in vivid checks, heavy boots, and gauntlet gloves. The men wear much the same, but in darker shades.

Everyone is heading somewhere, carrying something or dragging it behind them over the snow.

The familiar dogs have already appeared: two huge Alsatians, a ponderous shaggy Saint Bernard, and a few smaller dogs that sink into the snow as far as their bellies and derive enormous pleasure from it.

The snow shovels grate away, scraping the snow off the footpaths. Already the familiar sleighs bearing provisions are climbing at an angle, one drawn by the familiar donkey who likes bananas and the other, smaller one loaded with milk-cans, harnessed to a dog.

A distant low-lying slope already teems with skiers, who have their runs there and jumps built from piled-up snow.

Through our binoculars we can see them performing their leaps and overturning in reckless abandon—in helpless, desperate resignation, resolved thus to die.

They lie for a while in the snow as if never to rise again from their fall. Yet rise they do, gathering up legs, skis, and poles with their circular baskets. And move off again up the mountain—retracing this path of downfall and eternal return.

And in the cavernous depths to the right—in its smooth flat valley, walled in by jagged peaks—flows the dark, effervescent green water of the river Rhône, weaving its way between banks of snow, misted over by the brown mesh of riverside trees.

Now Miss Norah is calling *"buon giorno"*[8] to the Italian Signore Manlio Costa who lives on the floor below and enquires if he too is going for a walk. Yes, he too is going for a walk.

Everyone is going for a walk. Except the cheery Miss Norah who lies naked on her balcony in the sun.

For Miss Norah is confined motionless to her bed for the third year running, patiently waiting for the tubercular lesion in her hip-joint to burn out. And six months ago something started to affect her right knee as well.

She is cheerful, curious, sociable, and has so much time on her hands she is learning every language in turn so as to converse with friends from every possible nation. But she clearly lacks talent, since she can utter but a few words in any language and pronounces them in a most odd way.

And so once more a day passes—or maybe only an hour—and the men and women return home, swaddled in their patterned woolens, skis slung over shoulders, sleds at their feet. The spring thaw has cleared the roads. Water rumbles down the mountainside,

gurgles in ditches and drainpipes, pours along the guttering that
protrudes from the roof of our villa over the balconies and out
across the garden, washing away in the sun an enormous icicle
that hangs down the height of half a story and drips like a stalac-
tite onto a second, planted below in a tree, a freakish stalagmite
overgrown with black branches. That tree is forever destined to
bear its crystalline mistletoe—scarcely does one bunch melt in
the sun, when another begins to grow and spread.

Now the familiar donkey is on its way back down the mountain, pulling not the silent sleigh laden with vegetables but a
cart on wheels. And in the cart, the familiar dog with his daily
milk-cans.

Snow remains only on the high summits and slopes where
the sun never reaches. The billowing forests stretching below appear black to the eye. And the flat valley of the Rhône has turned
entirely chocolate-colored, its white froth melting as swiftly as
the cream on Wojski's platters.[9] Through our binoculars we can
distinguish clearly the lattice-work of fields and bare trees on the
banks of the black flowing water.

Miss Norah has just concluded her brief, unintelligible conversation with the handsome Señor Carrizales, the Spaniard
with a balcony on the nethermost floor, and is now calling to
Mademoiselle Hovsepian, who replies: "che, che."

Hearing these odd conversations, I get the impression the
people Miss Norah addresses don't fully understand her. But
Miss Norah, conversing in this way, always laughs gaily. And that
laugh of hers is intelligible to all.

4

The exquisite beauty of Madame de Carfort, who sits opposite
me at the dining-table, enhances all my meals.[10] I always imagine
her framed by two miniature azaleas standing among the dishes,
in a cold surround of white flowers.

She resembles the wicked Queen of the Ebony Isles, gold-embossed on the dark leather binding of *Stories from the Arabian Nights* lying on a table in my faraway home, where the Queen of the Ebony Isles always holds a leopard, golden like herself, on a short tight leash.[11]

So when I saw Madame de Carfort for the first time, I had the impression I'd known her a long time.

Hers is a *long* kind of beauty. And I should describe her in detail because everything about her is beautiful and unusual.

The languid, oriental gravity of her eyes, extended oval of her creamy face, stark, high forehead sharply defined by the black line of her hair, narrow aquiline nose, and stern mouth—yet a mouth able to smile with the most extraordinary delicacy.

Madame de Carfort is no fairy-tale woman, though she lives in an Arabian palace and has a maid called Fatma. The wife of a French officer stationed in Morocco, she drives across the desert in a car, attends parties at the homes of great Arab sheiks, and converses with their wives in the harem.

Madame de Carfort and Señor Carrizales are the most handsome people staying in our villa.

Despite her beauty and youth, Madame de Carfort is oddly severe, menacingly virtuous. Always simply attired, she barely exposes her neck even in an evening dress. Fastidious, haughty, and honey-sweet at the same time, she loves to discuss religious and moral problems. She is reading a life of Saint Geneviève, whose name she bears. Furthermore, she reads widely and has her own subtle, yet inflexible opinions on the things of this world and its beauty.

Despite her severity she knows how to respond to a joke promptly and aptly, knows how to laugh. But her laugh is always a kind of concession—a resignation from something far more important.

She takes pride in high French culture. One can talk for ages to her about the history of France, the Renaissance, or the era of Louis XIV and Louis XV. In the beginning, however, before I understood her sensitivities, her dark face would blush in angry embarrassment whenever I made some neutral remark on such topics. She complimented me on my knowledge, but would have preferred me perhaps to have been less well informed.[12]

She regards these subjects as untouchable, nothing but good. She's a Legitimist.

The new democratic and atheistic France, on the other hand, is an offence to her pride. She believes it will change but doesn't speak of it too candidly. She is shy about her love for her fatherland.

Once I realized this, I avoided sensitive topics, and derived great pleasure from our conversations about Pascal, Huysmans, Wyzewa, Mauriac, and even the life of Saint Geneviève.[13]

But another excellent partner in such discussions is not so delicate. Monsieur Totsky is a Swiss citizen with no clear memory of his Russian origins. Perverse, facetious, even malicious—he does not easily make concessions.

With him, Madame de Carfort—vanquished and disarmed by laughter—is momentarily at a loss. But her luxurious exotic eyes quickly become serious again, glowing all the more brightly as a result of the defeat sustained.

In contrast to Madame de Carfort, Monsieur Totsky is totally modern. A lover of the mountains' beauty, a passionate Alpine climber, he also proclaims democratic principles, is a republican. To some extent he even likes revolutions—though he's not too happy about the one that recently befell his former homeland.

Clearly, if "the gods" were thirsty for power a hundred years ago, then that was fine in many respects. But thirsty now, according to him, was another matter.

5

The first time I saw Miss Norah, she was hobbling on her crutches across the small sitting room at an hour when there was usually no one there.

She seemed to me small, plain, and no longer young in her warm, voluminous, blue dressing-gown, with her mane of red hair evenly cropped above the neck and her pince-nez resting on her short nose. She was as sunburnt as only country folk are at harvest time.

We were introduced by Mademoiselle Hovsepian, who was also present.

With a smile that revealed her long teeth, Miss Norah immediately told me all the Polish expressions she knew. Apart from *"dzień dobry"* and words to do with the weather, there was also: *"dosvidsjenie."*[14]

She also told me how happy she was to be still on her feet, because this was the last time. From the next day on the doctor had ordered her back to bed—for how long, no one knew.

So she was paying her farewell visits—exactly as if she were about to depart on a distant journey.

Just then she was on her way with Mademoiselle Hovsepian to visit the latter's compatriot, little Sossé—delightful, enchanting, unhappy Mademoiselle Sossé Papazian. Since Sossé never rose from her bed at all, she was saying good-bye before a much longer separation.

"Much longer," she said again. "No one knows for how long."

From the next day on Miss Norah would have no pleasure except receiving visitors. But she herself could visit no one.

So I said I would visit her. And she, laughing and thanking me, went on her way with Mademoiselle Hovsepian and her crutches.

A few days later I indeed went to visit her. But as I stood in the corridor outside her closed door, I hesitated whether to knock. I had spotted a large bouquet of red roses stuffed behind the door handle.

After a moment's reflection I retraced my steps, abandoning the visit. I preferred another of her friends, or simply one of the duty staff, to hand her the flowers proffered in such a strange fashion and watch the effect they had on her.

When I went a second time there were no flowers stuffed behind the door handle. I heard someone call out, but found no one in the room.

"Come on in, I'm here!" Miss Norah cried from the balcony.

The high bed covered in a quilt of bold floral design stood close by the balustrade. Miss Norah lay among the strewn pillows completely naked, roasted by the sun and in high spirits.

She was burnt a pinkish brown from top to toe, like a Creole. And was very pretty. So much so I was taken aback, so unexpected was her beauty after our first meeting. Her small dark breasts, rounded hands, slender contours of thighs and hips, tight belly—her whole body, sleek and swarthy in the sparkling sunlight, gave the impression of having been cast in bronze.

One needed to be aware of the slight deformity in her hip in order to notice it, a mere blemish on that bronze statuette. Her knee—the sickly one—still seemed the same on the surface as the other, small and perfectly rounded.

The attractions of her body were reflected in the beauty of her face, endowing it with an entirely different significance. Her green eyes, no longer concealed behind the pince-nez, looked at me joyfully from under her cropped mane of hair.

Miss Norah would shriek, laugh, and chatter away—animated, gay, enthusiastic, curious about everything.

Later I grew accustomed to her gaiety. But at that moment both her gaiety and bodily attractiveness seemed horrifying, almost scandalous, in comparison to her terrible fate.

When I sat down on a low cane chair, her whole person was thrust upwards along with the bed—and the perfect, hard dark contours of her body were thrown against the distant, icy, silver expanses of mountains and sky.

Thus she lay naked, surrounded by books. Berlitz guides to every language under the sun flaunted their bright red covers. In a large Dutch vase on the bedside table were yesterday's roses.

She showed me some small black albums in which she'd stuck heaps of Kodak photographs. Views of England full of memories still dear to her, images of family members, her friends, a pretty country cottage against a background of old trees. But some of the later albums held only photographs of the local mountains and the friends she'd made here, different groups of people in which she too appeared—always laughing. And finally a series of photographs of herself—naked. I had to admit they were very successful.

I also noticed that Señor Carrizales frequently featured in various combinations.

"He's handsome, don't you think?" she said.

"He *is* handsome—but what of it, what of it?" I thought to myself sadly.

But she was full of mirth. She loved to look through her photographs like this. In one shot she was still not so ill; in another, she was worse again. For a time she'd improved so much she was able to walk entirely without crutches, with just a cane. But later she suffered a relapse.

"When I look at them, I remember everything in turn—my whole life. And I find that very agreeable..."

6

Entering into something akin to friendship with the choucas, we doubted for a time whether it were anything more than an illusion of intimacy or merely a misunderstanding. Choucas are almost identical, so it occurred to us perhaps different individuals were coming every time and the ones we thought we knew, won over by our hospitality and remembering it, were not returning.

Our anxiety was groundless, however, because soon we had familiar choucas that we could distinguish from others.

One bird was crippled in the right foot in such a way that its toes—if one can put it like this—were constantly clenched into a fist. And it stomped around with this club foot as adroitly as any other bird with a normal foot.

For choucas do not hop like sparrows but strut like chickens—slowly, tentatively picking and choosing where to place their feet.

Once the one with the fist didn't appear for two days, then came every day following this break.

A second familiar choucas had a truncated leg—also the right—cut off near the top. This one could no longer stomp around, only hop on its healthy leg. But it held itself well, was quite sure of itself, and ate with a good appetite.

Not all have such good appetites. One, for example—or maybe it was several?—would sit on the balustrade, take something in its bill and spit it out, then pick it up and again spit it out. Eventually it would peck at another identical piece, hold it in its bill for a while and then swallow it with deliberation. It would stand on the balustrade a little longer and eventually fly away without eating anything else. Either it had a poor appetite—or perhaps too refined a taste.

Choucas are identical in appearance, but their temperaments are very different.

Some are so fearful they drop like thunderbolts from on-high, grab whatever they can in passing and vanish into the mountain chasms. Others—timid but greedier—cling to the edge of the balustrade and hang there, fluttering their wings with a sound like rustling straw. They peck avidly, scrambling to grab food from one another before they abandon the edge in terror and dive into the deep. Yet others stand comfortably side by side, feed for a long time in no particular hurry. Even when they have enough space, they thrust out their black breasts at their frightened companions, all aflutter and hanging on by one foot, and, with a firm shove of the right leg, cast them into the abyss.

Whatever they are like, strangers or friends, the choucas are always there.

It's foggy—and the black phantoms loom out of the ocean enticed by the food. Then the sun shines again—blazing, awesome, tempered by the reflected glare of the snows, accentuated by the blue-black recesses of crevices and slopes—and then the birds' glistening forms fall out of the radiant cornflower-blue, cheerful, chirruping, well-adjusted, likeable.

Usually they fly in flocks over the vast amphitheater of the valleys. But we were so high up, we saw them mostly from above.

If they chanced to be higher than us, however, then their approach, soaring and circling overhead, was wonderful to behold. Wings and tails outspread, a bird would resemble a cross of valor—its golden bill illuminated by the sun's rays, and its coral legs tucked underneath like jewelers' ornaments against the black enamel of its belly.

To glide, soar, or dive in free-fall at giddying speed against the deep azure of the sky—all are effortless feats to the choucas. For long intervals they do not move their wings and allow themselves to be borne by the currents—drifting in circles, parabolas, as though drowsy and bewitched.

But to land at last and stand upright on the narrow barrier where the bread lay—that was a real challenge. A choucas would arrive, cease moving while still in the air, hang as though suspended, hover, shift to right and left—until it eventually landed with great caution, sometimes to grab just a single crumb in passing, only to fall away again immediately without even regaining its balance.

The most difficult decision for them was whether to land when several other choucas were already sitting and eating—and so it was important to consider in advance where to land. Sometimes the clumsy descent of a single choucas caused such commotion it scattered all the others at once.

If a choucas hooked its feet onto the edge of the balustrade and ate in that position, then all that could be seen against the huge backdrop of mountains and air was its gentle black head and high, stroke-able shoulders; the rest would be hidden behind the balustrade as though it were sitting at table.

CHOUCAS

Thus Monsieur de Flèche would say of the choucas: *"ils s'attablent."*[15]

Monsieur de Flèche lived underneath us next door to Mademoiselle Hovsepian, and also liked to feed the choucas. But we couldn't treat seriously this competition from below. On his balustrade lay only ordinary breadcrumbs such as we kept on the floor for the sparrows. Monsieur de Flèche had no idea how "they liked it," no aspirations to learn how to pamper them.

With us it was otherwise. Great feasts would take place, sumptuous breakfasts, when apart from soaked bread and crumbled cake we would serve bananas chopped into fine slices, apple wedges, even walnuts. The choucas would descend in a whole flock, flapping their wings and hurrying, shoving one another, seizing the food and swallowing it any old way, hovering in the opening of the balcony, while the sky resembled a moving curtain—embroidered with black birds against a cornflower background.

There were also more intimate parties. Five to seven birds would settle along the balustrade with careful deliberation and surrender to the pleasures of the banquet. They would peck slowly at different courses, tasting each one in turn, nodding to one another with their smooth black heads as if saying: *"On mange bien ici tout de même."*[16]

And at last they would fly away all at once, calm, afraid of nothing—fly away only because they had eaten *"à leur faim."*[17]

7

One day at table Mademoiselle Hovsepian announced she knew how to prepare authentic Turkish coffee. And she invited us to her room to try it.

Mademoiselle Hovsepian is so thin and tiny it almost beggars belief. Always in mourning, she dresses only in black. She has black hair and great black eyes beneath thin eyelids, and wears

18

a black dress, black sweater, black stockings, and black slip-on shoes. Only her hands and her thin little face are white.

Señor Carrizales, who doesn't much like her, says Mademoiselle Hovsepian resembles a choucas. Naturally, in our eyes such a comparison cannot reflect badly on anyone.

Mademoiselle Hovsepian looks older than she is, like oriental women often do. Her eyes have a tragic frightened look, ready to weep at any moment—eyes that have *seen.*[18]

But whenever someone speaks to her, she smiles sweetly like a child. And that smile on her slender lips, revealing her dainty white teeth, is the only sign of her youth.

She is not suffering from any illness, doesn't cough or have a high temperature. But she is so slight, frail, and imperceptible, it's as though she only existed in part, so to speak. It is hard to believe someone could be so small.

When we crossed the threshold of her room, we were struck by how different it was from other rooms in our boarding house. The walls were covered in hangings from Oropos, the work of exiled Armenian girls. A beautiful faded, gold-and-violet rug covered the wide flat sofa and extended as far as the middle of the room. Low down on the wall above the silk cushions hung a small picture by Aivazovsky of considerable worth.[19]

For no one knows that Aivazovsky too was an Armenian!

Mademoiselle Hovsepian had lived in the mountains for several years and had no intention of ever leaving. She still felt most at ease in this hospitable country full of noble-minded people. Besides, she had never had a roof over her head anywhere in the world.

She showed us a strange elongated coffee-mill in which lay the coffee, ground by herself into a powder fine as dust.

We examined various small objects she valued as relics— old coins, old books written in the classical language known as Grabar, whose typeface resembled the runic inscriptions on a prehistoric burial mound.

She read us the titles of contemporary books, likewise illegible to us, names of poets and artists. Of all them she said "they were," for none was still alive. All the best, the whole flower of the Armenian intelligentsia had been wiped out.[20]

Mademoiselle Hovsepian was born in Trebizond[21] but no longer had family there. She had no one anywhere. She was alone. They had all perished. And how they had perished!

As a child she had heard stories of the terrible slaughter carried out by Abdul Hamid in Van, Mush, Bitlis, Diyarbakir, and Trebizond, of three hundred thousand murdered Armenians. And then after the Young Turk Revolution, from which they had expected liberation, of how new massacres had erupted in Adana and in Cilicia.[22]

We drank the Turkish coffee from delicate, little, dark-blue cups with gold rims, savoring the sweet aromatic powder in our mouths. But she went on:

"When the war broke out, new persecutions arose—and then one million, two hundred and fifty thousand Armenians perished. The Turks murdered them in their homes, on the streets, in prisons.[23] Little boys were rounded up in town marketplaces and slaughtered with axes and knives, while their mothers howled in anguish behind the police cordon and went crazy. Whole Armenian towns, whole armies of ghosts, whole hosts of those destined to die[24] were driven across marshland and desert, along the same routes where the corpses of those who had gone before lay festering. As they marched, they died of hunger and infection—men, women, and children. They stopped to rest in cemeteries, in the poison of bodies barely covered with soil. Then they walked on again, leaving behind those dying of typhus and cholera in the grass between graves, and where the cordon denied access to American and Swiss relief workers.

"Often, in the vicinity of towns, a hand or gnawed bone could even be seen, or pieces of decomposing human flesh, dragged from shallow collective graves by dogs. The waters of the Euphrates were poisoned, stinking of corpses…"

Whenever she spoke like this, her tragic eyes, storing within themselves the horror of what they had seen and otherwise brimming with burning tears, would be totally dry. Only her fine delicate lips trembled and twisted slightly when she closed them.

8

In addition to ourselves, an Armenian from Constantinople, Monsieur Peynirian, had been invited to the coffee party. Abandoning his homeland, he had been forced to leave behind his mother as well as *"une immense fortune,"* as he put it, because he had once conducted profitable trade with Baghdad and Damascus and owned businesses across the whole of Turkey. All he knew of his mother was that she had not yet died, but he could neither send her letters nor receive them from her. He himself had scarcely anything to live on. He was waiting—for what? No one knew. For new political transformations, the awakening of the international conscience, a miracle?[25]

All the promises made by America and Europe had come to nothing.

In vain had noble-minded Switzerland, Armenia's friend for thirty years, persisted in its efforts, appealed to institutions, governments, and parliaments reminding them of paragraphs of treaties that had never been enforced.

From the time of the Treaty of San-Stefano and the Congress of Berlin,[26] when the great powers had committed themselves to the defense of Christians in Turkey, until the peace treaty that recognized the independence of a new Armenian Republic in the Caucasus and proclaimed the annexation of the Armenian *vilayets* in Turkey—nothing had been adhered to.[27]

Monsieur Peynirian was not in the least like a Baghdad merchant of oriental tales, of childish make-believe, or the illustrations of Edmund Dulac. His rather ordinary face could equally have been that of a German, a Frenchman, or a Jew; his clothes were the antithesis of any hint of the exotic.

His unassuming appearance endowed everything he told us with the entirely unpremeditated character of total neutrality.

Armenia, he explained, living in slavery for eight hundred years and recently partitioned among Russia, Persia, and Turkey, had placed all her hopes in the victory of the Entente. Relying on the conscience of other peoples, however—believing the slogans in whose name the war had been waged—was a form of naivety that Armenia shared with many other nations.

From the outbreak of the war, Armenian volunteers had battled their way through to Tiflis,[28] fought in France, in Russia, and in Palestine.

But already in 1916 a secret pact was concluded according to which Armenia was to be divided among England, France, and Russia. Such was the design of those friendly powers as they voiced their demand for the liberation of peoples—and only circumstances beyond their control ensured it was never realized.

The occupation of Cilicia by French troops awakened extravagant new hopes among Armenians.[29] Hundreds of thousands of refugees returned from exile and, having the guaranteed protection of the occupiers, resettled in that part of the country with complete confidence. Meanwhile nationalist troops under Mustafa Kemal[30] soon entered Cilicia—and so the once-conquered Turks gained a victory over the previously victorious French, who then willingly extended the hand of reconciliation. And those Armenians who had not managed to flee were left to their fate, prey to fresh massacres in Marash and Hadjin.[31]

And so nothing had changed despite the great postwar world transformations. In 1918 the independent Republic of Armenia came into being in the Caucasus and two years later was absorbed by the Soviets, thus becoming, as before, a part of Russia.[32]

Here Mademoiselle Hovsepian intervened:

"Cilicia is the former Kingdom of Lesser Armenia. In the 11th century the Pope and the Holy Roman Emperor gave it to the Armenians as a reward for the aid they, as the only Christians at that time in Asia, provided to the Crusades. From the beginning of the 4th century, when Mazdaism was the dominant religion in the East, and the Greek gods were in the West, the state religion of Armenia was Christianity."[33]

Thus she spoke in her soft, shy voice of the great history of Hayastan, of its old culture and language,[34] its beauty and its heroic and tenacious survival throughout eight centuries of slavery. She spoke of the splendid basilica in Ereruk, of the former capital of Ani at the time of the Bagratuni dynasty, conquered by the Turks and destroyed along with the marvelous shrine to Saint Gregory dating from the 7th century.[35] She told of the great wars her people had waged against Assyria, Persia, and the Romans.

Yes—this small black-clad, almost invisible Mademoiselle Hovsepian was the daughter of an ancient people, a descendant of the Hittites of whom the Bible speaks. And she loved this homeland of hers, a country that had existed for two-and-a-half thousand years.

Monsieur Peynirian was leafing meanwhile through a book he had taken from the many-sided low table standing before the ottoman. When Mademoiselle Hovsepian stopped speaking he requested permission to read us a couple of passages.

One was a copy of a secret order issued by the Turkish Minister of the Interior in 1915:

"[...] it is urgently recommended that you should not be moved by feelings of pity on seeing their miserable plight; but, by putting an end to them all, try with all your might to obliterate the very name 'Armenia' from Turkey. See to it that those to whom you entrust the carrying out of this purpose are patriotic and reliable men."

The second passage went as follows:

"Doubtless you appreciate the confidence which the Government has in you, and you realise the importance of the work entrusted to you. You are not to permit one single Armenian to remain in Bab.

Your severity and promptitude with regard to the deportations can alone assure the success of the scheme we are pursuing. Only you must take care that no corpses are left by the roadsides. [...] The lists of deaths sent to us recently, are not satisfactory."[36]

Having read this out, Monsieur Peynirian was silent for a while. But he told us later: "I once happened to see a strange piece of jewelry. It was a rosary, intended for prayer, of which the beads—larger ones for the Our Father and smaller ones for the Hail Mary—were made from dried nipples, from the cut-off breasts of murdered Armenian women..."

At the very end of this conversation Mademoiselle Hovsepian intoned her characteristic refrain: "One nation should not oppress another, n'est-ce pas?"

9

Like everywhere in the world, so too in our villa there was one affair that was much more interesting than any other and the subject of discreet observations, muffled conversations, sneering remarks, and speculative inquiries. It was—put briefly—the sensational private drama of Monsieur and Madame Saint-Albert.

The couple arrived after the rest of us and sat at their own separate table in one of the rooms linked to the dining room by wide-open doors.

Three walls of this room were made entirely of glass and partially draped in diaphanous white curtains. A single monkey-puzzle tree stood as high as the ceiling alongside a host of flowering plants. I don't think I'd ever seen such tall geraniums with such magnificent branches and pink blooms the size of whole bouquets. Azaleas and cyclamens blossomed in the corners. Whether in full sunshine, when the warm light streamed through the glass panes and curtains, or in the evening, when the lamp burned beneath its gold silk shade, this flower-filled room gave the impression of a truly enchanted place.

Madame Saint-Albert was tall, attractively dressed but no longer young. She had fine, largish, well-bred features, a cold expression on her lips, and a cold stare. Occasional wrinkles—on her neck, around the eyes—were not immediately visible. Immediately visible however was her icy manner, her habit of staring as if from afar, as if from another shore: her whole style of being a woman who no longer feels she counts, no longer desires to suggest anything to anyone.

There was nothing about her of what might still uphold or prolong youth—not even a fleeting glance or smile.

Looking at her, I thought with approval that this was a woman who knew how to grow old in a timely manner.

Her companion on the other hand—for some reason, no one called him her husband—was a young man who required no artifice to flatter his youth.

Señor Carrizales maintained with typical self-assurance that they were definitely not a married couple, although he was not acquainted with them personally and knew nothing about them. He trusted to his intuition, which told him that Madame Saint-Albert, despite appearances, was a *grande amoureuse* who had abandoned her husband to travel far from society with this beautiful boy.

No one really believed Carrizales. He succeeded nevertheless in sowing doubt.

Indeed, the intriguing couple did not seek the company of others, apparently sufficient unto themselves. They seemed happy together—both were healthy, enjoyed sport, and were constantly going on outings. We encountered them on the ski-runs, in the tea room, at musical concerts—always together.

Everywhere she maintained her characteristic gravity, or lethargy. She was a woman of few words. He bore instead the whole burden of conversation. He truly did everything he could—always good-humored and full of high spirits, always full of his youth.

Monsieur Saint-Albert did not possess the astonishing good looks of Carrizales, but he was certainly a handsome man.

His smile could quicken the heartbeat not only of a woman of forty. It was hard to avert one's eyes from such a smile. An unusual physical peculiarity, pure coincidence, meant that the way his teeth were set, or perhaps the exaggerated fullness or consistency of his lips, caused him difficulty, undue effort, in smiling to the end, to the full—I don't know quite how to put it. But this smile was enough to bring about tragedy.

His gallantry, his attentiveness to her every wish, his clearly demonstrated feelings created the impression he was seeking her pardon for something—in face of her coldness. Just for being younger? It was all to no avail. Even that smile of his, his own special smile, was powerless. Always between her beautiful brows there lay a deep furrow of hardened gravity.

Sometimes when she poured out his wine or put something on his plate, he would kiss her fingers fleetingly in the air without trying to catch hold of her hand with his own.

Yes, the sight of these two left a disturbing impression.

Each of them separately might have been happy in their own way. The remnants of her beauty—the beauty of *artistes* or women of fashion, whose youth can be prolonged for a long time by people's indulgent consent—might have brought a few more years of happiness to someone her age.

Indeed—it was an odd affair and gave us all food for thought.

Whenever Monsieur and Madame Saint-Albert left their flower-filled room and walked across the dining room, they were escorted to the stairs by everyone's stare.

Even stern Madame de Carfort raised her long, black Arabian eyes in that direction.

10

"She must have suffered a lot."
"So you're not enjoying it, like last time?"

"No. Last time, I disliked the taste for quite different reasons: more a certain dryness of character, pedantry, Calvinism maybe…"

"You mean that?"

"The rigidity of her principles, her life agenda. But today's bird must simply have had difficult personal problems, family or emotional."[37]

"Only because you took the leg. Other bits are quite tender."

Such was the way one conversed with Monsieur Totsky, sitting at the dinner table and carving the slightly tough turkey-meat off the bone. One never knew what nonsense would occur to him as an appropriate topic of reflection. His wit preyed on everything, craving to utilize it.

At the table opposite, framed by clusters of white azalea, the head of Madame de Carfort could be seen.

She wasn't looking in our direction and said nothing, though she was listening to our conversation. She simply let herself be seen. And that was already a lot.

After dinner we went into the lounge to listen to music. Monsieur Totsky, as usual, played everything he was requested—from Beethoven to Poulenc to shimmy.

Everyone was in high spirits because Monsieur Est had come downstairs, deathly pale in his scrupulously maintained black attire. He was very ugly, however, and looked more like a Samoan than a Jew. He was the youngest among us and reduced us all to hysterics with his inexhaustible good humor. Even Lady Malden, always terribly shy and serious, watched him sympathetically, as she crocheted a long chemise out of coffee silk chiffon.

Monsieur Est had not fared especially well in his native country, Romania. Antisemitic incidents among the students had forced him to leave the university in Bucharest. He had been continuing his law studies in Paris when ill fate had caught up with him. He contracted tuberculosis, from which his mother and two elder brothers had already died.

He was supposed to be seriously ill and not allowed to leave his bed. But his reckless desire for fun and rejoicing meant he paid no heed to his doctor, and from time to time appeared among us unannounced. He would play the piano, sing, dance, joke, and even flirt—showing special regard for the beautiful and inaccessible Madame de Carfort.

His ideas were on the level of student pranks, typical of his age.

A notice had been hung up the previous day in various locations in our villa requesting the residents, because of a shortage of water, to use it as sparingly as possible.

What a blessing that was for Monsieur Est! He proved endlessly resourceful in devising ever-new sacrifices, restrictions, and penalties connected with the water shortage. Moreover he drafted his own series of similar announcements and posted them along the corridors, wherever it was possible to affix them with drawing-pins, ostensibly in the name of the management:

"The management requests persons with high temperatures to inform the administration, so that the extra warmth can be harnessed to heat the radiators."

"Due to Sister's excessive workload, the sick are requested to summon her only in case of dire emergency, namely at death's door."

"In order to contain infection, the management kindly requests patients to refrain from spitting on the ceiling—both inside the building and outside its walls."

There were many more such notices, but I failed to memorize them.

A genuine victim of Est's humorous exploits and somewhat childish impertinence was Madame de Carfort. Annoyed with herself, she would laugh nevertheless, the fleeting red glow on her creamy face making her doubly enchanting.

This time, she was scandalized when faced by his low bow and request to dance, and reluctant to agree. But at last she consented and deigned to dance with him—with that too cheeky, ugly, and unhappy boy. Maybe she did so out of pity—or perhaps because he was indeed the best dancer and even she found it hard to resist the temptation.

In the end she too, like the others, had had enough. They forbade him to dance further and ordered him back upstairs. He knew how to win hearts, however, and was permitted to stay provided he behaved with greater composure.

He sat down at a small table on which a bell-shaped, glass dish cover stood on a metal tray, and armed with pencil and fork, he improvised jazz rhythms to the dance tunes played by Monsieur Totsky. And when the sounds of pencil against glass and fork against tray were no longer sufficient, he struck the table-leg with Lady Malden's crochet hook, making a delicate, flat, high-pitched twang, like the whine of a mosquito.

He played his instruments proficiently, with the ardor and musicality of a poor Jewish dulcimist.

Eventually he took his leave of everyone, but lingered longer by Madame de Carfort in order to hum for her—no one knew quite why—what he claimed was a "topical" song by Tosti: *Mourir c'est partir un peu...*[38]

And at that moment he looked like a comical, pathetic, macabre dwarf standing beside his princess.

When he had finally departed, Monsieur Totsky rose from the piano and went over in turn to Madame de Carfort.

But she frowned at the sight of him in a manner visible to all. Then Totsky asked whether the company and wit of Monsieur Est were really more to her taste than his own.

Madame de Carfort explained in a cold dignified tone that she did not make such comparisons. However his attempt to interpret the stringiness of the turkey by making fun of religion, even such a religion as Calvinism, seemed to her far more tasteless than all of Est's foolish jokes put together.

11

Monsieur Totsky appeared not to respond and after a while resumed his seat at the piano.

As he began to play, the Saint-Alberts unexpectedly entered

the lounge accompanied by Mademoiselle Hovsepian and Monsieur de Flèche, our neighbor from below who also fed the choucas.

Monsieur de Flèche was a tall man over thirty with bright delicate features and very fair hair.

Enticed evidently by the music, the Saint-Alberts were making their first appearance here and, as usual, created an impression.

They sat in the deep armchairs near the entrance and listened in silence. Carrizales, who was already present, immediately occupied the place next to Madame Saint-Albert while Mademoiselle Hovsepian came over to join us.

"They are a married couple after all, Monsieur and Madame Saint-Albert," she said under her breath, addressing Madame de Carfort in particular. "They're a married couple, but married only recently."

Madame de Carfort stirred uneasily. I also felt uneasy: something too serious was indeed going on between those two.

"Monsieur Saint-Albert is the nephew of her first husband," added Mademoiselle Hovsepian.

She had learned these details from Monsieur de Flèche, who ate his meals in his own room and was rarely seen. He had known them previously or perhaps heard of them earlier. In a word, our doubts were unjustified, and as usual it was Carrizales's fault.

But Carrizales did not feel in the least bit guilty. As soon as the music broke off, he began to entertain the company with extraordinary verve and enthusiasm in his impeccable French.

I heard him call—not for the first time—Blasco Ibáñez a *traître* and a *bandit* and speak resentfully of his book on Alfonso XIII. Monsieur de Flèche expressed surprise that such an excellent writer was so detested in his own country, and Carrizales promised to give him a book to read on Ibáñez by El Caballero Audaz.[39]

He once lent me this book too—a weak and indiscriminate polemic, in which the most powerful accusation against Ibáñez was that, having choked on his false teeth, he called for a doctor and thus proved his lack of courage.[40]

Yet Carrizales found it convincing.

How that exemplary Spaniard burned with admiration for his king, his general,[41] and his beautiful, poetic fatherland!

Madame Saint-Albert watched him gravely, but her cold grey eyes did not perceive at all his charming good looks. With such an expression on her face she could equally well have been listening to him as thinking about something completely different.

The light from above fell almost directly on her large placid face. Illuminated in this way, two crescent moons of tiny wrinkles were so vividly emphasized beneath her eyes, it was embarrassing.

In contrast, her young husband gazed at Carrizales with all the intensity of his lively, impressionable attention. He surveyed him from top to toe, simply savoring and enjoying that magnificent specimen of the human race.

Meticulous to the utmost in his clothes and manners, irreproachably aesthetic and well-bred with long, dazzlingly white teeth and flaming brown eyes, Carrizales was indeed worthy of notice.

A fervent Catholic who attended Mass every day, went often to confession, and the only one at our table observing all the fasts, he was a loyal son of the burgeoning Spain of old that once threatened the equilibrium of the world—the Spain of inquisitors and crusading knights, the Spain of fanaticism and glory. There was a time when, having conquered the Turks in the East, she ventured into Africa, fought the Protestants in Germany, France, and England, converted the idolaters of the New World, forced out the Jews and Moors from among her own, and refined the fiery passions of her faith in the embers of the autos-da-fé.

Today—dwarfed and of little significance—Spain had been fighting ineffectively for years the mutinous leader of her part of Morocco, sending ever more gold and troops to their doom.

How natural it seemed to the impassioned Carrizales that Spain should go on fighting—go on sending people and money—

until the incomprehensible criminal resistance of the rebels was broken.

We listened to all this from a distance. And this time the naive words of Mademoiselle Hovsepian, spoken in a low whisper without her looking at anyone, felt even stranger:

"But one nation should not oppress another, n'est-ce pas?"

Her tragic eyes peered out questioningly from her small, sharp, absolutely white face.

Madame de Carfort watched her coldly and did not respond.

But when Mademoiselle Hovsepian had departed, she turned to me and said: "These Armenians are quite intolerable. They bore us all with their misfortunes."

I confessed that, in the last resort, their misfortunes didn't seem to me so boring.[42]

She smiled her precious smile, so full of delicacy.

"We may have something to say about that. Did you know the occupation of Cilicia cost France two and a half million? And yet they were butchered again afterwards."

12

I am surprised to see I've mentioned Monsieur Totsky several times but not mentioned at all what he looked like. However, I think I should do so now.

After all, a person's outward appearance is usually very important. Not just their dimensions and coloring, but also tiny details of their bearing: a gesture of the hand, the posture of the neck, a smile—these are expressions of the inner nature. Such apparent trifles are as if the means by which nature attempts to reveal itself, discreet efforts to make its voice heard at any cost.

Meanwhile, when I try to describe in writing what Monsieur Totsky looked like, I simply have nothing to say. His whole appearance was so odd and insignificant that it gave nothing away and put the man himself under no obligation.

Please believe me when I say that Monsieur Totsky's having blue or black eyes was a matter of complete indifference both to him and to others.

By nature, he enjoyed making jokes, for instance, yet his facial expression was totally unamused—but neither was it entirely sad. Instead it was a bit bored and rather sour, but that too is an exaggeration—because he simply had no expression. He loved sport, would hive off into the mountains for a several days at a time, had the reputation of a first-rate skier—yet lacked the air of being physically adroit, as he was neither tall nor well-built; nothing about him was memorable. He was also phenomenally musical—but who would have suspected it on hearing his high-pitched voice or his unpleasant, slightly nasal, drawling speech?

He also tended to make unnecessary gestures more foolish than he was himself, expressing a kind of contentment with God knows what. Whenever he bowed, he straightened his back with an exaggerated movement; whenever he picked something up, he gave it back with an extravagant sweep of the hand, almost with reverence.

No one could do anything to change the way he was—it's hard to explain even where the problem lay, or of what he fairly could be accused.

To be sure, there was a lack of inner harmony, a disturbing disproportion in his bodily and spiritual make-up. And my objections might indeed be a little "flimsy" were it not for the fact that everyone else also felt a certain awkwardness in relation to him, though no one tried to investigate its nature.

If I mentioned his lack of success one evening with Madame de Carfort, then it was precisely for this reason. I am sure the matter of the sinewy turkey and its Calvinism was secondary—it was more about everything taken together, which meant Monsieur Totsky was bound to lose out in any comparison.

Est, for example, was very ugly and certainly too familiar, and almost dying to boot. But in him, everything seemed to somehow hang together and cause no one embarrassment.

That said, I can now speak of one of our joint trips up the mountain—though it was no genuine mountain expedition.

Except before I do, I must mention one other thing.

Namely that at those altitudes, amid those snows and frosts, in addition to the scorching heat encountered in sunnier places at certain times of day, one other thing took us by surprise—and that was the extraordinary warmth indoors.

The majority of guests slept by open windows, while the patients kept their windows open day and night. Meanwhile all the corridors, staircases, larger rooms, and common spaces were so deliciously warm I can still recall to this day the impression they made on me. Even in rooms permanently ventilated, it was enough to shut the window for fifteen minutes for the air to grow warm and cozy.

The air above the radiators constantly quivered and vibrated, while the whole villa belched forth its heat, mingling with the icy fragrance of the snows and cloying aroma of roses and carnations.

13

And so one day we went for a walk in the company of Madame de Carfort and Monsieur Totsky to a particular spot in the mountains from where there was a view over Lake Geneva.

We climbed uphill, but the mountain was so steep it was hard to breathe. We followed a narrow path, made slippery by sleds and skis as it zigzagged across the slope.

Every so often we paused gasping for breath, and looked behind us. Ah! Every hundred paces revealed fresh enchantments. In the crisp frosty air, above the high snows that had been three days in the falling, the magnificent local sun made its way across the deep blue sky. A single cloudlet had again attached itself to the summit of the Chamossaire, but this time it remained there motionless for a few hours, so still was the air. The white summits and ridges, especially the north-facing, were brightly illuminated and sharply delineated against the intense dark blue of the sky, sprinkled with sparkling snow, like sugar. Likewise spruce forests—packed with fluffy snow—stood out against the sky on ridge tops as in a spectroscope. All the valleys, slopes, and recesses were a distinct navy blue—in sharp contrast to the surfeit of radiance and luminosity.

The frozen surface of the snow scrunched underfoot; there was a nip in the air. We were walking through a wood where every tree was as if white-washed, weighed down by snow, its many lower branches rooted in the piled-up drifts, the upper ones entangled in other trees, a sight worth seeing. Lesser bushes, their crests submerged, thrust out single black branches from under the banks of snow.

Again we paused, puffing and blowing, and again we surveyed the same view—through wide-open arches in the forest, like "lights" between trees—only more splendid, more expansive, as the valleys sank ever deeper into the abyss.

We walked to one side of the path as skiers or small sleds flew down the slope, shooting past us at ever more reckless speeds. The bob runs started lower down where the path was wider and not so precipitous.

We passed ski and toboggan runs, panting for breath as though from hard physical labor, but still the path did not come to an end. We followed the deep tracks of some wide heavy runners—like those of peasant sleighs back home. But here there was no trace of a horse's shoes between them, only the prints of large hobnailed walking-boots.

The forest now stretched only below. To the right of the path there was nothing but the naked whiteness of obliquely lying snows.

We walked on like this for another half hour, along the upper rim of the forest, pausing and laughing from exhaustion. Between the tracks of the runners the snow was now breaking up, like ice. But the mountain air, hard from the cold, gave us strength. And again we went on without feeling the strain, dragging our legs out of the snow as we sank up to our knees.

At last we reached a small plateau, seeming to end in a rocky ridge. But there was still some way to go to this ridge.

To one side, on the verge of the forest our path stopped. Here, covered in snow, lay piles of wood chopped into logs, and by one of them stood the big sleigh with no animal harnessed to it that had shown us the way thus far. A large, grey-haired, old man was loading the logs onto the sleigh.

Monsieur Totsky urged us to keep going across the snow. But the woodman, seeing our hesitation, told us that it was not far to a place from where we could also see the lake. Monsieur Totsky wasn't keen on the idea, but eventually we followed the old man.

We sank into the snow up to our waists, but it really was closer that way. Somehow we eventually reached a low barrier protruding from the snow.

We stood and stared.

Below us we caught a glimpse of a green sky between clouds, and below that another amphitheater of mountains—and through the dark scattered shreds of clouds, a deep brownish valley in the foreground, bathed in sunlight, and then in the middle of the valley the immense bright surface of the lake stretching far into the distance to the right—like a vast expanse of concentrated light.

And there was the river flowing into the lake, its banks and mouth outlined in dark colors—everything sharply delineated and unreal like on a relief map.

The grey-bearded man had already left us and returned to his work—embarrassed and surprised to receive payment for his services.[43] Whereas we remained transfixed, gazing at the world below, at that living map, intersected by roads and tracts of forest, dotted with little towns, whose scale suddenly shrank when we removed the binoculars from our eyes.

Eventually we'd had enough, and it was time to return. And so we retraced our steps, glancing around carelessly at the nearby slopes, forests, and escarpments.

Here was nothing but stillness, deathly silence, and ruggedness. Above a bare incline bordered by a ridge of forest, a few choucas were circling, gently chirruping.

We looked down from above, however, because something had caught our eye. Untouched elsewhere, the snow in this secluded clearing was covered in bluish markings—ruts clearly made by skis but quite different from those on the regular runs.

Yes, something was there on that white patch between the forests—as if someone had drawn it. A bizarre inscription in giant letters. Who on earth could have fought through those woods and whatever for?

"Well, exactly!" Monsieur Totsky suddenly said in his irritated high-pitched voice, and simply walked away from us toward the woodman as though he had taken offence at something.

We, on the other hand, familiarizing ourselves with what we observed, read out letter by letter the colossal inscription laboriously etched in the snow with a ski blade.

It ran at an oblique angle to us, downhill, toward the valley. The first letters were enormous, but the rest grew gradually smaller. They were not joined up but separated by great leaps, yet retained the dot over the "i" and grave accent for the "è". The final full-stop stood on its own at a distance, like a star, huge—absolutely enormous. The inscription spelled out the name of Madame de Carfort's patron saint: Geneviève.

Madame de Carfort, sullen and red in the face, was the first to avert her eyes. Even here amid the snows she never ceased to look like an oriental princess—in her white woolen hat resembling a turban and brown tricot tunic with its gold and sapphire zigzag design.

We returned without saying a word in the direction of the sleigh, which was already visible, and of Monsieur Totsky, who was talking to the woodcutter. No, this was not an appropriate way to demonstrate one's feelings, although very few people could have guessed in fact who did it and whom it concerned. But we belonged precisely to that number. And Madame de Carfort was clearly distressed and even humiliated—all the more so perhaps because we said nothing, aware nevertheless of everything.

But what were we supposed to say? Precisely such a tasteless mixture of romanticism and schoolboy humor was typical of Monsieur Totsky.

The old man had already loaded his sleigh as high as he could, yet still fastened a bundle of larger logs to a towrope at the rear of the sleigh.

We had imagined he was from the nearest cottage, which we had left far below on our way up, and that he had come up here to gather wood for himself. However, it was quite otherwise. This old man earned his living by transporting wood to the clinics to heat the stoves—to the clinics that lay the furthest down, twice as far down as our own villa.

"And you do this every day?" We were amazed considering the man's age and the steepness of the path.

"Every day," he replied. "This is the fourth time I've been up today."

"Fourth time?" This really did beggar belief. Yet he was hoping to return one more time.

"*Ça m'fatig' pas beaucoup,*" he said. And smiled, accepting a cigarette.[44]

He seated himself with great care, almost solicitously, on the low fore-carriage of the sleigh in the great shadow of the fruits of his labor, small and insignificant beneath that huge pile of wood.

He showed us his heavy hobnailed boots. As he traveled down the mountainside pursued by that enormous weight, he had to use them to control the momentum, which would otherwise carry him away and crush him to death.

He dug in with his boots—and the sleigh moved forward. With a grinding, grating, and scraping of wood and snow, he was gone from our sight in a flash along with his vast, shifting, living pile of logs.

He was gone—but in my thoughts was immediately transformed into that delicious warm air quivering and vibrating above the radiators.[45]

14

At the hour when residents of our villa usually paid each other visits, I went again to see Miss Norah. The weather was cold and damp, the eiderdown of mist hung outside every balcony—and Miss Norah was lying inside her room in the more usual fashion, in bed and under the quilt. Now she was not so pretty again, but not wearing the pince-nez.

By her bed stood a small table covered in an embroidered white napkin and on it a vase of roses, percolator of black coffee, and bottle of liqueur.

Miss Norah was not alone. On the far side of the table sat Señor Carrizales.

This time no books lay on the flowery quilt. They were piled up instead on the marble top of the bedside cabinet.

Ah! How loudly and heartily Miss Norah laughed as Señor Carrizales held forth about the beauty of Spain with his customary enthusiasm and gesticulations. Miss Norah was finding it terribly hard to follow him—while allegedly making use of his impeccable French, he in fact uttered every word in Spanish.

For my part, I had the impression they understood one another perfectly well despite such difficulties.

Señor Carrizales—spirited, distinguished, exotic—grew handsomer still from enunciating those magic names and sounds. He endeavored to recreate for us the essential charm of the Alhambra, or the wildness of his sierras, or the Easter processions in Madrid when women from all walks of life put on national costume and, veiled in black lace, stepped from sun-drenched squares into the gloomy naves of churches.

He indeed had the means, despite everything, to make himself understood.

Having drunk my coffee, I judged I was free to depart. But Miss Norah wouldn't let me go.

Lady Malden came in and likewise received coffee and liqueur. When Mademoiselle Hovsepian arrived, however, the coffee had run out.

The conversation again turned to the gravely ill young Armenian, Mademoiselle Sossé, whom I had not yet met. Mademoiselle Sossé translated Armenian songs and was a writer herself. It would be a fine thing if I could meet her.

They always spoke of her in this way: Mademoiselle Sossé, or: little Sossé, as if they were discussing an amiable child. Everyone was concerned about her health.

Whenever I passed by her door in the evenings, I always encountered a row of flowers—azaleas, roses, cyclamens—standing on the floor in the corridor, removed from her room for the night.

Mademoiselle Hovsepian told me simply that little Sossé had herself requested we visit without fail.

"She hasn't got up from her bed for two years. She's not just sick. Maybe it's not so bad with her lungs—but it's as though her entire organism had lost any instinct for life. She too left Turkey, fleeing from the massacres. She was brought to Geneva as a little girl, to a boarding school. Before she left however—she had seen. Except with her, you can't talk about it at all."

"Yes, yes," said Miss Norah. Laughing, she went on: "I haven't seen her for a long time, because she can't come to me and I can't go to her. She's never been downstairs, never sat at table with the others. Whenever the doctor permits her to get up and walk across the room, she faints. And yet she isn't so very ill…"

I arranged with Mademoiselle Hovsepian when I should go. Meanwhile Carrizales was showing the other women a beautifully illustrated Spanish magazine. There were faces of actresses, generals, toreadors. And then photographs from the battlefields in Morocco. Carrizales explained it all to us, slipping again into his customary enthusiasm so full of charm.

"Do you know, ladies, what they want? That Abd el-Krim, those Rif republicans?" His magnificent eyes were burning. "They want—independence!!"[46]

15

Of all the hotels and sanatoria in our colony, the Palace stood on the highest ground. It was the loveliest and largest. Everyone knew it was there, though it was actually invisible. Only on walks and excursions was it possible to see a fragment of roof or one of the higher wings, and in the evening watch an enormous glow spread over the forest from the lights burning in all its windows.

Concerts, shows, and other entertainments were staged in its conservatory, known as the *Jardin d'hiver.*[47] It was possible to reach there on foot by climbing the steep zigzagging paths— and it always seemed as if we'd lost our way since nothing suggested the proximity of people. We'd still be having doubts as we ascended a stone staircase set in the wooded mountainside, sheer like a ladder. At the top of the staircase, an immense far-reaching terrace bordered by snow-bedecked spruce suddenly appeared before us. At its far end the Palace rose up, leaning almost against the massive cliff—tall and very wide, with its glazed windows shining bright, its huge entrance also made of glass. A corpulent attendant stood by the door in navy-blue uniform adorned with gold buttons.

But it was also possible to get there by the grumpy electric cog train.

Always protesting quietly under its breath, the train would leave our station and immediately plunge into the gloom of a tunnel. The flat, edelweiss-shaped electric lamps eternally burning on the rocky walls only emphasized the obscurity. It would climb steeply upwards in the gloom like a slow, unwilling, yet obedient beast.

At last, without warning, it would emerge out of that massive, gigantic, totally sheer wall of rock into the bright world above upon whose summit, seeming to touch the sky, stood a small, black spruce-wood covered in snow.

Directly opposite the little station where we alighted, the back wall of the Palace rose up, two stories lower here than at the front. A small footbridge conducted us across the void and straight onto the second floor. We had to descend two floors to reach the conservatory.

Vast vestibules, corridors, lobbies, reading rooms, rooms for drinking tea or listening to the radio, a rich library, a concert hall—everywhere was laid out with plants, full of light and space. Invisible pipes of hidden radiators distributed a delightful warmth within the confines of this sanctuary, while the frosts and snows of the mountain night continued to harden beyond the great glass panes.

A rampart of forest below the terrace blocked off the view over the mountainside, which was studded with villas and usually ablaze in the evenings with bouquets of light. Nothing could be seen except immense ravines, gloomy forests and mountain ridges, forbidding in the moonlight. Steeped in purplish-blue light, the cast-iron sky sealed in this entire world beneath a layer of shifting clouds. One had the illusion of being totally cut off from life, a sense of menacing disorientation and loneliness— while the huge hotel of a thousand rooms teemed with tourists from all over the world.

In this wild place on the lofty heights, it was strange indeed to stumble upon such warmth, luxury, and elegance.

Stucco pillars divided the room into various nooks and alcoves, while hanging palm leaves screened off these quiet havens. Armchairs of various shapes and sizes waited invitingly around the low tables, able to indulge any whim for repose. Seductive music emanating from a grand piano, cello, and two violins induced a state of breathtaking intoxication. It was possible to imagine that life was beautiful and infinitely diverse, that it was possible to live long and always be happy.

At my side sat Mademoiselle Hovsepian and Madame Saint-Albert. We were a large group. Apart from our usual friends there were the two agreeable Russian women, from whom Monsieur Totsky kept his distance. Carrizales, on the other hand, kept close by. I overheard Monsieur Peynirian telling shy, serious Lady Malden about the rosary beads made from the amputated breasts of Armenian women. Monsieur Saint-Albert was sitting beside Madame de Carfort who, as so often happens with flawlessly beautiful women, looked less stunning than usual in a hat, which modernized her exotic head. In contrast, the rigid profile of Madame Saint-Albert gained from being framed by a little, black, silk bonnet.

Mr and Mrs Vigil, the young English couple, exhausted by their day-long outing, almost lay across two gigantic, oval leather armchairs. The quartet played some old French dance. Silk-wrapped electric lamps shone with a friendly glow. The tranquil warmth lulled everyone into a heightened state of languorous well-being.

Madame Saint-Albert replied to Mademoiselle Hovsepian's questions in a low whisper. When the music stopped, I caught the following words:

"I do not look at life, *I look back at it.*"

She said it with emphasis, in a dry voice, hard like her features.

"There's no real deliverance from our errors of judgment," she continued, staring quietly at the shiny surface of the table. "Nothing can be put right now, nothing changed. Now it's clear it was meant to be like that, and not otherwise."

I saw Monsieur Saint-Albert, who was conversing with Madame de Carfort, suddenly glance toward his wife, but not with his customary tenderness, rather in alarm. But she did not notice.

"Yes, it's just a horribly disappointed form of curiosity, to finally receive an answer to all the questions asked of life. That's as much as can be said—nothing more and no two ways about it."

Tea, cream cakes, and pastries were served. Mr Vigil was drinking a cocktail and urging his wife to do likewise.

This cheerful, powerful, broad-shouldered Englishman was entirely larded, so to speak, with lead. He had strange markings on his face and temples, even on one eyelid. We had seen his x-ray, where masses of little white spots of lead could be seen embedded in the skull and eye-sockets, collar-bones, and shoulders.

One of his rabbit-shooting companions had released a whole round of shot into him from a distance of a few feet. Not without pride, he told us that, after eight months of lying on his back, his first outing had been to hunt rabbits. Mrs Vigil nodded to indicate it was indeed true and this was precisely what her husband was like.

The music stopped playing. But somehow no one stirred from their seat. There was still plenty of time until supper. Hushed conversations continued at other tables. Young women with clipped bobs and fringes sat on round sofas, dressed only down to the knee, yet rendered strangely eloquent and graceful by the exposure of their cheerful, slender, variously positioned legs. There was an awful lot of women's legs about then, almost naked, always more resplendent than their dresses. It was hard to believe—confronted by such sophisticated, luxuriant shapeliness—that but an hour ago they had been trudging up a mountainside in the snow, clad in thick stockings and heavy boots, or flying past on their skis, muscles straining, tendons taught as wood.

Young men sprawled in armchairs or perched unceremoniously on the armrests, and amused the women with their jokes.

Older ladies occupied with their needlework or gentlemen of leisure indulged the young people good-naturedly.

On either side of the long mirrors, monkey-puzzle trees stood many feet high. In the vast conservatory, translucent from so many glass doors and windows, the uppermost leaves of giant palms reached into the high-vaulted ceiling crowned with its cupola of stained glass.

"It's a disgrace to be old," Madame Saint-Albert suddenly said. Since she was addressing Mademoiselle Hovsepian, it was possible not to respond. But everyone who heard these words felt embarrassed.

We finished our tea and made ready to depart in the general commotion. And in that commotion I heard again the voice of Madame Saint-Albert:

"It's just as troublesome, just as awkward socially, just as shameful as poverty."

16

The two Russians who attended the concert with us at the Palace did not live in our villa. They came to us only for meals and often to listen to music.

Apart from their language they had nothing in common, and possibly didn't even like one another.

The elder of the two, nearing thirty, had a withered face, deeply marked by anxiety over political matters. She constantly sought news from Russia in all the daily papers, was in touch with various Russian émigré factions, lamented their decline in spirit, and had her eyes perpetually fixed—across the great divide of mountains and continents—on the deep interior of her vast, lost homeland.

She never spoke about herself. But it was obvious that, apart from the general calamities, she had also experienced private ones. She was a divorcée or widow who had lost family members, probably in tragic circumstances. But, as I say, because of her sad and secretive disposition, nothing was actually known. Usually in conversation one had to adopt a subdued and sympathetic expression. She had a German surname: Wogdeman.

One aspect of her plain, insignificant exterior attracted attention and even inspired reflection: her eyes. It seemed as though they'd sucked the whole intensity of their color from her grey face, pale lips, faded flaxen hair, and concentrated it within themselves. They alone were dark—of a brownish yellow, almost russet hue, completely dull and lustreless. Framed by thin eyelids and set wide apart, they were not only sad—and I would say, homesick—but also unbelievably distant. She was always gazing as far away as possible: when out walking—at the horizon, when indoors; beyond the window at least.

The other Russian, Mademoiselle Alice, in contrast to Madame Wogdeman, was distinguished by her great candor. It was difficult indeed not to know something about her. After all she was scarcely twenty-two and life had not yet taught her the merits and privileges of discretion.

She was tall, slender, and willowy. One always caught sight of her immediately—she somehow stood out in the distance. She laughed with full, seductive lips revealing her many magnificent white teeth. She also wore a long, dark plait she couldn't bear to cut off, despite the dictates of fashion.

Mademoiselle Alice created around herself an aura of erotic turmoil. Anxious to preserve her good name, she was continually trapped in some awful state of indecision. At the same time, however, she literally could not tolerate not being threatened by something.

Fortunately for her, something always threatened. And only this constant state of anxiety guaranteed a form of consolation.

At the time when I became *au courant* with these matters, the danger had just been averted from a Monsieur Curchaud, a resident of her villa, who had proved to be a man entirely unworthy of her trust, frankly not a gentleman. And now there emerged, as the next alarming problem, Monsieur Peynirian.

Thus far, however, Mademoiselle Alice was not fearful. On the contrary. She even put forward the idea that Armenians from Turkey differed very much to their advantage from Russian Armenians. Fine. I was more than willing to believe it. But Monsieur Peynirian, crushed by his fate, so far-removed from his "great fortune" and especially from his fairy-tale Damascus, didn't seem to me in the least attractive when seen from this angle.

I'd hardly glanced round, however, before Monsieur Peynirian was no longer the center of her attention. I couldn't establish whether he'd betrayed her confidence or was entirely unworthy of it, but Mademoiselle Alice was now asking me whether it was possible that Monsieur Saint-Albert, so young and handsome, could really love his wife, who was so much older than he and even quite plain.

Already initiated to some extent into her doubts, here is what I unexpectedly heard:

"I'm in an awful position," she said in all earnestness. "It's that Vianelli, the black-haired, rather fat Italian who's often with Costa. I only found out yesterday, even though I run into him every day because he lives on the same floor. I'm scared of everything. He has such a crazy nature. Just think: an Italian! He says he's in love with me, that he liked me from the first moment. He had suggested we go tobogganing together, and so we went. He squeezed me a bit too hard but I pretended I hadn't noticed, and we arranged to meet in the evening at the dance-hall. Naturally we returned together. He promised to escort me only as far as my door. But later on, when we were already upstairs…"

Well, naturally, he wasn't worthy of her trust, of which Mademoiselle Alice still had so much with respect to the world. Only her determination and unswerving severity made him finally leave.

He told her that no woman before had made such a power-ful impression on him. And Mademoiselle Alice believed this explained a lot of things.

"But, my God, someone might have overheard us!"

Such fear on her part was all the more surprising since she told me everything—me, who had overheard nothing.

Another time she confessed to me she was very upset because she'd had her final conversation with Monsieur Saint-Albert. She had beseeched him by all he held holy not to pay her any atten-tion, not to compromise her. She reminded him of the obliga-tions he had toward his wife, despite her age. With total sincerity, she told him of the strange effect she had on men, the mystery of which she couldn't understand herself, and warned him of the danger lurking inside her, independent of her will. Eventually she implored him to take pity on her, who was there without family, without protection, and begged him not be her undoing.

"But he's a hard man," she added begrudgingly after a pause. "He must be very self-possessed. I have no idea what's really go-ing on inside him. He barely said anything the whole time, only smiled ironically. But I got him to a point where he eventually thanked me for my warnings and promised he would avail him-self of them. Do you think he'll keep his word?"

I was too little acquainted with Monsieur Saint-Albert to hold any opinion.

And I should also stipulate, as a general point, that if I repro-duce here Mademoiselle Alice's confidences, then it is not be-cause they especially mattered to me.

And I am not ruling out the possibility that I'm not even always accurate in my account of the actual facts, that I'm sometimes mistaken as to the persons who came into play—although I always listened to Mademoiselle Alice's words with the keenest attention.

This was because the thing that struck me most in her confi-dences was what they had in common, what typically and invariably repeated itself every time: a specific pattern of perpetually shifting equilibrium between defeat and victory. Her need to arouse passion in men was just as strong and irrevocable as her need to triumph over it.

These extremely aggravating—so to speak—circumstances, these affairs of a most dubious nature, acquired a different connotation and value according to her dialectics; they had their own higher meaning and praiseworthy goal.

Mademoiselle Alice made me stop and reflect precisely because a certain paradox of woman's nature found expression in her—if not its most perfect expression, then perhaps simply its most extreme.

And so one of the men—let's say the handsome Carrizales—is pursuing Mademoiselle Alice. She allowed him to kiss her on the stairs only once, and he immediately imagines God knows what. Not long after, he escorted her home from a concert and again tried his luck on the stairs. In great indignation she told him he mustn't think it would always be so easy as the first time. She scarcely managed to prevent him from entering her room. In fact, he did come in, but only for a moment. She told him to leave at once. But before that, after she'd already lain down, because she was very tired, he sat down on her bed, on the quilt, and, taking advantage of her vulnerability, began to kiss her. As he kissed her he told her (he too!) that no other woman had made such a powerful impression on him…

At this point Alice's narrative becomes so involved and complicated I'm not even able to reproduce it precisely. One thing is certain, however: it is only here her real triumph begins. Namely because in all these doubtful situations, something crucial had been saved, rescued. Some last sentry-post, some ultimate bastion of resistance had held its ground; some prey had been found to satisfy her unyielding womanly self-respect.

I find it difficult, as I say, to penetrate the elusive subtleties of such self-flattery, but I remember with absolute certainty that when Carrizales, on the express demand of Mademoiselle Alice, finally quit her room, she managed to utter these words too: "You wouldn't have behaved in this manner if you had any respect for me." And after that Carrizales avoided her, not daring to even look her in the eye...

Yes. All this material evidence, which she assembled before my eyes, was supposed to demonstrate her ability precisely to resist—precisely her inaccessibility, precisely her uncompromising womanly pride.

17

One Sunday afternoon we decided, come what may, to explore what went on in the village. Madame de Carfort wished to come, so did the Saint-Alberts. And Mademoiselle Alice, overhearing, said she too would join us, but first she had to drop back home to change her clothes.

The plan was to go dancing in the restaurant of the Hotel Toscana, where the lower echelons of local society—hotel porters, lift-boys, shop girls, and quarry workers—congregated to amuse themselves.

For us it was not a total novelty, because we had spent the initial days of our stay in this very same Toscana.

Our first refuge in this country had indeed been extraordinary. Entering the hotel's interior, we passed a spacious and elegantly furnished dining room, where a pianola played unflaggingly irrespective of the time of day. The owner of this sanctuary, a fiery, muscular Spanish woman with a thick mane of black hair, would dance there with her guests—before noon in her dressing-gown, in the afternoons in a jumper, and in the evening in a revealing, low-cut, brightly colored silk dress. The waitress serving the tables, an Italian with long gold earrings and a gold band across her dark forehead, would dance alongside her mistress in free moments. Finally the man of the house, likewise a Spaniard, young, slight of build, and calm headed, took no part in the dancing; instead, he played billiards with the guests in another room off to one side.

Meanwhile, the children of this Spanish couple played under the billiard table—two black-haired little boys with placid temperaments and melancholy eyes.

When there were no guests, the mistress of the house would stand in her negligee by the great dining-room window and intone one-steps in her warm juicy voice, as she stared through the tulle curtain at the white mountains in the distance. Her placid husband, concealed somewhere behind the bar, would accompany her on a mandolin.

Thus their life went by, one might say, "in song."

Sometimes, however, the mistress would tear herself away from such pastimes and disappear into the kitchen for a quarter of an hour, in order to personally supervise one or another of the long list of dishes on the menu.

On our first evening we succumbed to the temptation to try some of these. The first course consisted of nothing but green lettuce dressed in olive oil, while the second, which was warm, also provided much food for thought. It consisted of rice, green peas, finely sliced sausage, and bits of fish.

When we enquired, highly discouraged, what this meant, the Italian waitress with the gold band and gold earrings explained it was simply—*olla podrida*.[48] She looked at us so endearingly with her soft black eyes that we had to content ourselves with this answer.

Having nowhere else to go since all the other hotels and pensions were overbooked, we tarried for a few days in this atmosphere, which was not without its charms, in a stylishly furnished room with many mirrors and a floor that was never swept—despite our chambermaid being a German. But she explained that instead of cleaning our room, she had to stand in for her Spanish mistress in the kitchen, even though she'd not been engaged as a cook and had no idea what she was doing.

Thus it was to this odd place we decided to repair one Sunday afternoon to drink tea "with toast" among people dancing to the relentless music of the pianola.

And so it came about. Though there was no "toast," only cakes.

We entered at a moment when no one was dancing. All the tables were occupied. But at the far end of the room Mademoiselle Alice caught sight of us and leapt briskly to her feet. Still in the doorway, we all saw her simultaneously, so tall and animated in her gestures, standing out so distinctly against the backdrop of her surroundings in her close-fitting black-and-green dress and little black hat pulled down over her eyebrows.

She was in the company of Monsieur Curchaud (though well aware by then that he was not a gentleman).

We walked over to join them, to take advantage of their invitation and table.

The landlords greeted us like old friends while the Italian took our orders, pushing back her disheveled locks, dislodged behind the gold band by dancing, and surveying us as before with her endearing gaze.

When we had all sat down, Mademoiselle Alice found herself beside Monsieur Saint-Albert. But she paid him no attention, talking to everyone in turn, except to him. Eventually, leaning across the table, she busied herself exclusively with Monsieur Curchaud, who sat further away.

Monsieur Curchaud had arrived from Indochina to spend two weeks enjoying winter sports among the snow-covered peaks. His forty years had taken their toll on the otherwise perfect physique of the tennis and hockey "champion." A slight corpulence around the waist and back of the neck detracted from the grace and freedom of his movements. In spite of this he was a first-rate dancer and showed much enterprising spirit. He was smooth-mannered and good-humored, and talked readily and interestingly. His still young eyes, black and slanting, and a bald patch above his forehead made him slightly resemble a China-man.

The conversation turned to opium and naturally to Farrère.[49] So, was it as he described? So, had it come to this?

Monsieur Curchaud approached the matter with forbearance, regarding Farrère's book simply as a literary work.

"People treat opium as if it were a big issue," he said with a smile. "In fact it's less harmful than alcohol, which no one makes into a political question. First of all, it's only rich Chinese who can afford to get high. Furthermore, the bad effects of opium aren't hereditary like those of alcohol. The harmfulness of opium ends with the addict. The new generation is free of it…"

The pianola was playing again and a few couples were dancing on the small surface fenced off by rows of tables. Among them was the Spanish landlady dancing with a tall strapping Italian, a worker from the local quarry. Now I understood why she danced for days on end. She danced magnificently—with the intense, raw solemnity of passion, with the firm rhythm of her full hips, with the muscular dexterity of her short sturdy legs. She placed her left hand flat against the back of her partner's neck just below the hairline, and with the right pulled him into the orbit of the rhythm with odd jerky movements, shedding nothing of that raw solemnity.

She performed that popular international dance, executed those familiar steps and paces in a way exclusive to her and, de-spite everything, exotic.[50] She would stealthily follow the steps of her casual partner and then make a bolt backwards, lean to-ward him for a split second, and immediately pull him towards her again—nimble and strong, muscular and adroit, solemn and frantic.

We watched only her and talked only about her. She was the true queen of that smoky ballroom.

As she danced, she was also watched by her two calm little children sitting on the floor in the shadow of the billiard table.

Only Mademoiselle Alice paid her no attention. She was making fun of Monsieur Curchaud for some reason—more or less because he didn't always succeed in achieving what he wanted. She was urging him to pluck up courage to have a dance—and absolutely, with *la patronne*.

"As we're here, we ought to enjoy ourselves with them. Why don't you have a go, since she dances so well?"

But Monsieur Curchaud did not wish to dance. Such exoticism held no attraction for him, who had been resident in the distant colonies for over ten years.

Instead he asked Mademoiselle Alice to dance. Initially, she reacted with indignation, but eventually rose to her feet and wove her elegant silhouette in amongst the ring of dancers.

They had barely performed a few steps, however, when the Spanish husband, standing until then by the bottle-cabinet behind the bar and keeping an unruffled eye on everything, flung himself upon them and attempted to part them. We watched this scene, which did not seem to surprise anyone except ourselves, in astonishment. They too were outraged and protested their right to dance like anyone else. But they relented when the Spaniard explained politely that the police never allowed more than four couples to dance at once.

They returned laughing to their seats and awaited their turn with impatience. And Monsieur Curchaud spoke again of his Indochina.

"Yes, yes," he agreed with some truism uttered by Madame de Carfort, for whom the problems of the colonies were likewise close to the heart. "Prohibition on the smoking of opium is impossible, absolutely impossible. It would cause such an economic shock to the country, like revolution…"

Before the music started again, Monsieur Saint-Albert leaned over toward his wife and whispered something in her ear. He looked at her for a moment with his enigmatic, intoxicating smile until she smiled imperceptibly and nodded in assent.

When the pianola struck up, Monsieur Saint-Albert quickly rose to his feet and invited *la patronne* to dance. She accepted this honor with dignity and immediately placed the palm of her hand round the back of the gentleman's neck, as she had done a moment ago to the strapping Italian, with the cold gesture of a wild-animal tamer.

Once again we watched their accomplished dancing—all except Mademoiselle Alice, who had managed with Monsieur Curchaud to secure a place this time among the four permitted couples—and she too impressed us with the grace of her posture and ethereal fluency of her movements.

18

I must confess we amused ourselves at that time rather better than expected and celebrated the end of the carnival season in festive style.

Besides, no one planned or even anticipated anything. We dispersed as usual after dinner, everyone going their own way. But later in the evening, toward midnight, when we were already preparing for bed, we heard a strange scratching on the door—like that of an enormous rat. I even took fright not understanding what it was.

After a pause, the scratching began again and then again, more impatiently this time. Finally, when we shouted *"entrez,"* the doors flew open and a completely rigid figure dressed in top hat and frockcoat entered, but with an empty black hole instead of a face.

It was a puppet on a stick the height of a man, carried by Monsieur Est, who was singing a short song about the Carnival prince in his croaky voice outside the door.

He had already assembled a considerable crowd of fellow guests in the corridor. And he warmly invited us to go downstairs where the *mardi gras* celebrations were about to commence.

He himself was disguised as an apache gangster[51] and looked intensely ugly with his uncombed mop of curly hair, scrawny neck wrapped in some shred of a scarf, and ghostly white face. He had bedroom slippers on his feet and a smoking jacket directly over his white silk nightshirt.

Carrizales, dressed as a toreador in his own pajamas, was assisting him with the preparations.

At our end of the corridor, in the milky-white light of the frosted wall lamp, several strange figures stood huddled over the banister, which began there, laughing under their breath so as not to disturb the sick. They had already visited Miss Norah and little Sossé, whose door was easily identifiable from the rows of flowers standing in the corridor, removed from her room for the night.

We all greeted each other again, because we were all renewed in the sense we'd changed our appearance. Although Lady Malden, for example, looked just the same as ever and Mrs Vigil simply wore a dark navy dressing-gown covered in gold stars and a gold hairnet in her hair—everyone understood all was meant to be nocturnal costume.

On the other hand, it was hard to recognize Monsieur Totsky attired in a sailor suit that was both too short and too tight—he looked like a little boy. Madame Saint-Albert was likewise completely transformed in the magnificent costume of a marchioness with enormous grey coiffure and stunning jewels.

Meanwhile from the far end of the corridor there approached a glittering golden sultana in dainty sandals and wide baggy pantaloons fastened at the ankle. Est removed his cap and bowed low before her as a sign of deep respect.

I did not realize immediately that it was Madame de Carfort.

Neither did I realize immediately that the tall figure of an Arab clad in white turban and floor-length burnous concealed the person of Monsieur Saint-Albert. It looked as if he'd simply wrapped himself in a soft white bath towel.

We were about to go downstairs when suddenly, alerted by the noise, the brother of our proprietress—young, cheerful, hard-working Charles, who was loved by everyone—came running up the stairs toward us swiftly and silently. He was the one who kept the whole place in order—assisted his recently widowed sister in everything, managed the staff, looked after us at mealtimes, and if necessary, carried our heavy suitcases upstairs.

Guessing what was afoot, he raised his eyebrows in horror while his long, comical, childish face assumed an expression of deep disapproval. For a time he tried to persuade Est to call it off, but Est threatened him with a bottle of Asti he'd been carrying under his arm. At the sight of this, Charles clasped his head in both hands in a gesture of blank despair, then mounted the banister and in the twinkling of an eye shot down the stairs to the very bottom.

He had acquired this skill even before he became *le garçon d'étage*,[52] serving as a sailor in the French fleet. It was his outgrown sailor suit that Monsieur Totsky had borrowed for the evening.

Monsieur Totsky followed Charles downstairs—not via the banister, but down the wax-polished steps, sitting as though on a sled and descending the awkward track without too many bumps.

The rest of the company descended in the usual way without encountering any hurdles.

In the lounge we found Charles already dressed as a page, bustling about with napkin in hand and a tray on which he brought us wine and various sweetmeats—cakes, a cream gateau, and fruit. In all this there was not a single doughnut or crusty fried biscuit.[53]

And so we imbibed Est's wine from crystal bowls on long stems, munched nuts and Malaga raisins. The party was first-rate—entirely spontaneous, without rhyme or reason. Totsky and Est played music—we danced a little, but only briefly. Then the national performances began. Carrizales enacted a bull-fight, inviting Monsieur Saint-Albert to participate as the bull,

to which Saint-Albert willingly agreed despite being supposed
to be an Arab. But of course this stood no chance of success, if
only because no one wanted to mimic the horse or the picadors,
apart from Est. So Carrizales explained as best he could that this
gave no idea of the real thing, which was so glorious. Then Est
danced an apache dance, but was immediately forbidden, so he
declaimed instead an erotic poem in Romanian with great earnestness. Then Mademoiselle Hovsepian recited a national bal-
lad in her own tongue, explaining how very beautiful it was. No
one understood a word, but everyone listened intently. We were
drawn especially into the mysterious obscurity of the sounds,
which contained for those who understood them immeasurable
depths of association and unimaginable charm.

Only Monsieur Totsky, who had no feeling for the exotic and
understood not a word of his forgotten native language, resisted.

"C'est horrible," he said rather boorishly.

So the party ended again with music, which did not pre-
clude conversation. And Madame de Carfort—different and
somewhat unreal in her sultana's costume—whispered something in response about her Morocco. She pined for it as for a
second homeland.

Only Est listened with hostility. Yes, for him it would have
been better if Madame de Carfort had had no yesterday, if she'd
begun only on that day and were to end tomorrow—just like he
was about to end.

As I observed this party, a moment occurred when I imagined they were all like children. Unprotected and exposed to every danger. So alone, and left to their own devices in this alien
mountain house amid the snows. Who was to keep watch over
them? The proprietress of this respectable old villa—a cook's
widow who had been asleep for hours? Or little Charles, who
had feared the nighttime commotion and was now making the
most of an opportunity to enjoy himself?

Who was responsible here for the whole show? No one.

Even Lady Malden had gone upstairs deliberately to fetch her crochet hook so that Est could play his jazz.

It so happened I found myself sitting beside Madame Saint-Albert, who looked so beautiful in her grey coiffure and stylish pink silk dress covered in bouquets of flowers, as though for this one evening she had dressed up not only in the marchioness costume, but in her own youth.

I told her of the strange impression I'd had, of my anxiety imagining that we were all—healthy and sick, young and old—a collection of thoughtless children, confronted by the seriousness of life, for whom no one was responsible.

She was silent for a moment staring ahead of her with eyes half closed.

"I don't know," she replied. "I do not see life. I look back at it, a long way back—and I don't see, I am no longer able to see..."

19

Suddenly the weather grew warmer. Water again drummed in the gutters, streamed along and across the roads, flew into the air from the pipe protruding above our balcony and washed over, as it fell, the strange icicle that had taken root in the branch of a tree I had described earlier as looking like mistletoe.

One could walk through stretches of forest which in shadow were still white, like in winter. But in sunny exposed places everyone thought spring had arrived this time and was here to stay.

And so too, it seemed, did the chaffinches. On that same day they flew up to our balcony for the first time. Everywhere we could hear them singing their brief, animated, always identical song—the very same as in my faraway home overlooking the meadows.[54]

The sun shone, the choucas ate their breakfast, Miss Norah was calling "Good morning!" to everyone, and we went out to buy newspapers and glue to stick photographs in our album.

On the way we passed various familiar things and persons.

Before us in the valley to the right we could see the flat roofs of villas and hotels located there, their names writ large on their roofs in letters legible from afar, or even seeming to hang in the air. I knew by heart all those *Beau-Séjours, Beau-Sites, Gentianes,* and *Belvedères* and could see them with my eyes shut—without even understanding properly the nature of the intimacy that bound me to them.

Mademoiselle Alice was walking on the road below, an utterly minute figure from where we were—in the company of Madame Wogdeman, it seemed. And deeper down still, in the vicinity of the giant vaults supporting the viaduct of the grumbling railway, Vianelli was clearly standing beside Costa.

We turned off behind the church, and the scene disappeared from view for the time being, while the most urgent thing became two rotating postcard stands displayed on the pavement outside a shop. Inside, beyond the windowpane, Monsieur Totsky was as usual purchasing sheet music.

A bit further on, we exchanged greetings with Madame de Carfort and Lady Malden at a point where bundles of walking sticks, bound together like lictors' rods, stood likewise for sale on the pavement beside sleds and skis stacked against a wall.

Madame de Carfort informed us that things had got worse for Monsieur Est, that things were very bad indeed. And we parted in front of three glass tiers of cakes at the entrance to the nearest tea room.

Later on in the glass fronts we saw hoards of sweaters and knitted woolen jumpers, then rows of monstrous alpine walking-boots, and later again skeins of wool in every conceivable color. Eventually we came to a shop selling glass and Dutch porcelain vases, all the more significant because of the two little glass cabinets standing by the door. There, on the shiny mirrorlike glass shelves flocked innumerable tiny choucas carved out of wood and painted red, sapphire-blue, yellow, azure, with black stripes or yellow spots. There were bigger ones and smaller ones, yet all deliberately made out of proportion, with enormous yellow bills bigger than their bodies.

Once I'd stopped in front of this cabinet, it was difficult to tear myself away.

This time we were joined by the Saint-Alberts and examined together for a moment the lamentable choucas. He laughed with his merry, happy laugh as he discovered likenesses to certain people in those avian caricatures. Yes, Carrizales was right, they were like Mademoiselle Hovsepian. Mademoiselle Hovsepian—and also Mademoiselle Alice.

I was astonished, since there was no true likeness at all between choucas and Mademoiselle Alice. And Madame Saint-Albert observed that every choucas had a different expression.

Then we agreed on one thing—it seemed as if spring was on its way.

Everything I have described so far took place on the right-hand side of the road. On the left side there was nothing but a barrier—and beyond it the steep slope fell away with its scattered clumps of trees. And now those same villas and hotels that we had passed only a moment ago also appeared flat from above and, in turn, showed us only their roofs or golden legends suspended in the air.

Our own villa was now among them, looking no different from on high to any other. While the familiar inscription, located on the side, now seemed unduly extravagant.

How strange the vanity of humans, who regard their own tent—however temporary—as the center of the world!

In the bright sunlight and ubiquitous dripping water, we made our way further up the mountain, as the road wound upward in sweeping hairpins encompassing ever higher stories of the slope. In many places, mud was already emerging from under the snow. Smooth expanses of exposed rock turned redder from so much water but, as they dried in the sun, again grew rosy-pink.

At a particular spot on the road we saw, as usual, Monsieur Verdy, a muscular old gentleman who always took his constitutional by walking back and forth here in the hours before lunch. He had his stretches of road marked out according to the bare wayside trees—and everyday had to walk a bit further uphill without stopping or panting.

He had made up his own mind to do this and never let a day pass without his training.

We compared newspapers and talked a little about politics. Yes, there was always something new to say about those Germans. And in particular and in private—as it were—about our very own German, Herr Fuchs.

Monsieur Verdy would joke: "Today I'm in luck, because I've not yet encountered that ape, Fuchs."

Monsieur Verdy liked to speak his mind and air his views. He indulged in blunt, strong language. Moreover, whenever he was about to hold forth at table, Madame de Carfort's mouth would assume in advance an expression of forbearance and disgust.

He was undoubtedly a resourceful and venerable old man. Well-versed in wines and tobacco, he appeared equally well-versed in life.

That day Monsieur Verdy was of the opinion it was going to get warmer—and on that note we parted company.

But further up the slope we bumped into the Vigils returning from on high; both had skis slung over their shoulders. They had not taken the thaw seriously and changed their daily habits. Higher up the mountain everything was still frozen and the ski-runs excellently preserved.

And it transpired that the chaffinches were wrong.

That very afternoon everything became engulfed in thick cloud. Heavy snow fell in the evening, and the next day we woke to the sharpest frost we had yet encountered. The air became still and palpable like solid glass as a result of the freezing temperatures, sun, and whiteness. Spruce trees, their branches weighed down to the ground, stood without the slightest tremor in their dazzling white mantles. The intense blue of the sky provided a hard backdrop to the distant summits, which seemed blown—like glass—out of silver.

The sun warmed the surface of the snow and by evening a hard crust had formed.

The chaffinches sat on branches where the snow showed no inclination to slide off, plaintively reciting their laconic song. What were they to do when the mysterious command of instinct no longer allowed them to return to the valley? They had absolutely nothing to eat in the frost and snow that had caught them unaware.

On our balcony lay the bread we'd prepared for the choucas. How was I to explain to chaffinches in the forest that we had food for them there? How to show them the way?

Yet after a few days of the freeze, a single chaffinch appeared on our balcony and perched on the balustrade. For a long time it didn't realize what it was, hadn't expected such good fortune. At last it stabbed at the food and after that fed unceasingly, for a quarter of an hour at least. How starved and frozen it must have been!

At last it flew away frightened by something. But a moment later returned to eat. And that same day flew in for a third time.

I thought it had clearly remembered and would return the next day and bring with it other starving chaffinches.

But it never reappeared.

20

Monsieur Verdy truly did think, believed entirely seriously that Germans were somehow different, and worse than any other people in the world. To him it was an axiomatic truth that didn't require proof, something immediately obvious that neither instinct nor reason could doubt.

Thus he gave the impression he very much needed, for some reason, to believe it.

And so it was.

Monsieur Verdy was our great friend. We were genuinely fond of each other.[55] He questioned us in great detail about our country, in all sincerity even. He was interested to know how many Poles there were—and very pleased to learn there were so many. Because, according to the latest edition of *Larousse,* the total population of Poland was only fifteen million.

It was then that negotiations were taking place with the English beside Lake Geneva, which were disagreeable to the French.[56] Every day we read lengthy reports on the talks carried by the newspapers. We were entirely of one mind in our concerns and anxieties.

Monsieur Verdy also didn't like the English and projected his dislike without hesitation onto kind-hearted Lady Malden and good-humored, congenial Mr and Mrs Vigil. But this was nothing compared to his hatred of Germans.

Yes, the Germans were indeed our greatest common enemy. This made us brothers to some extent in the eyes of Monsieur Verdy,[57] we were close because of that hatred. And that hatred overrode all other reasons and motives for our friendship.

Naturally, I had to agree with everything he said. Yet at the same time I couldn't resist the thought that the brotherhood of two nations consists precisely in the fact that they will unite against a third.

And hence the brotherhood of all nations, all peoples, would seem impossible. For *against whom* will they unite?

But I refrained from mentioning this to Monsieur Verdy, so as not to offend him.[58] And because he took a genuine, keen interest in Poland, unlike our other well-disposed friends.

Until eventually he asked:

"Well, and so, if things turn out as they want, if France were to be drawn in—then how many troops could Poland put up?"

The question was an unpleasant one. And for the first time I responded to Monsieur Verdy coldly, reluctantly, saying I had no idea.

But later I understood—understood why it was necessary to Monsieur Verdy for the Germans to be the worst nation in the world.

Once we met him again at the usual spot on the mountain road where he did his training. That day he couldn't manage a longer stretch without gasping for breath. On the contrary. The week before he'd run out of breath after completing only a very short stretch, and even had to sit down on a bench. He was agitated.

He told us how he remembered this road, these mountains from his youth. As a student he had spent six months on a cure and completely recovered. More than forty years had elapsed since then.

He showed us the view with his hand:

"Oh, there was nothing here in those days, only the bare mountain and the forest. Where the Palace Hotel now stands, there was a tiny boarding house, a simple wooden chalet. And down below there were a few other boarding houses. You had to travel up the mountain from the lake by road, by omnibus, and there was only one hotel, now also completely rebuilt. I would never have recognized the place—even the mountains seem different..."

That same day after dinner, Monsieur Verdy brought downstairs a photograph of his grandsons to show us. Two handsome, beautifully dressed, almost identical little boys with cropped hair and cockades on their collars; two little boys of whom there are multitudes throughout the world, all looking exactly the same. But these two—they were the grandsons of Monsieur Verdy.

We examined the picture and said what was necessary.

"They are orphans," said Monsieur Verdy after a while.

We assumed sympathetic expressions.

"My son is no longer alive, my only son…"

And then we heard another story, of how—in the fatherland's hour of need—his son had left behind a thriving factory, said good-bye to his parents, his wife, and these two little children; how no one had foreseen, or perhaps everyone had foreseen a little—and how Monsieur Verdy's son had never returned from the Marne.

How he and his elderly wife traveled a long way every year to visit their son's grave, how it was possible now to exhume and transport the remains…

Now I looked with different eyes upon that old man, who knew all about tobacco and liqueurs, loved to tell jokes, and be-grudged himself nothing in life. His bulging brown eyes were clouded by tears. Red blotches spread over his forehead and clean-shaven cheeks.

Yes, he had lost his only son. Only daughters remained. He had lost his son, who had already taken over the factory man-agement, enabled him to enjoy the sweet taste of retirement and guaranteed him a peaceful old age. When now…

Until the death of his son, Monsieur Verdy had been a healthy man. Only then did he lose his health—and that was why he had come back.

Now I understood. How could the Germans have murdered his only son if they were not the worst among nations? What sense would his son's death have if they were just the same as ev-eryone else, just ordinary people—if the mortal struggle against them were not the highest and ultimate imperative, if it were not God's explicit command?

21

The youngest of the Armenian exiles, Mademoiselle Sossé, was twenty-two years old. Yet her tiny, dark head peeping out from the depths of her bed, from among the feather pillows and eiderdown, seemed that of a little girl.

She had taken up residence in that vast bed many months ago in a practical and businesslike manner as if it were a little house. Beneath the pillows she had two electric buttons and could ring for assistance almost without moving, and also switch on and off the lights throughout the room.

Her room, exposed by virtue of its huge window to the beauties of the local scenery, was full of flowers, books, and playthings. Large and small silk dolls, dogs, monkeys, and little imp-like figures hung suspended on strings and rubber bands over her bed so she could easily reach them.

On a shelf close by she had folders of reproductions—photographs of people, countries, and paintings.

Books, of which she read piles, could not fill every hour of the day and night. Thus she often lay alone for long hours rotating some little figure, doll, or picture in her fingers. Sometimes it was those painted wooden choucas with their out-sized bills, sometimes an ugly porcelain cat, sometimes a tiny, naked baby also made of porcelain.

In this way she somehow coped with, managed, and reconciled herself to her fate.

In her short life she had indeed read a great deal—and as a result had grown sophisticated, sensitive, and wise beyond her years.

She had also experienced a great deal—and some of it she remembered only too clearly, some of it unimaginably terrible. Everyone knew that whenever she was in the throes of high fever, suffering in delirium, she would see a single monstrous vision known only to her, which filled her with terror and despair.

Her family lived in Persia. Once I witnessed her strange, tearless sobbing when she received a letter from her mother, whom she had not seen for ten years.

Everyone was fond of Sossé. People often talked about her—the one among us who was always absent. She had been poorly for a long time yet everyone continued to have faith in her recovery. From time to time she had violent recurrences of high fever. And then, any improvement achieved by whole months of cure would be lost in a matter of days.

Her youth, her peculiar spell, charmed both men and women. Mademoiselle Hovsepian, Madame de Carfort, and Madame Saint-Albert would come bearing news and gossip, attempting to smother with gaiety the sorrow gripping her heart, as well as her fear. Monsieur Totsky—always ironic and provocative—used entirely different vocabulary when speaking to her; he was gentle and benign. Monsieur de Flèche would banter with her in a voice trembling with the deepest, most tender emotion.

She would open wide her fearful light-brown eyes as she took to heart meaningless jokes and reproofs, and defended herself against imagined rebukes that no one had intended.

She possessed a grace whose measure and intensity is rarely granted to anyone. She sculpted every word she uttered with her own peculiar diction, dressed her soft singsong voice in a strange melody. She spoke sadly and playfully at the same time, with the capricious smile of a little woman already aware of how to manipulate feelings. And when she spoke, she would open wide her amber-colored eyes, staring at people with an astonished, timid sweetness. She greeted anyone who entered her room with this same stare, joyous yet full of trepidation.

It was always cheerful, welcoming, and magical in her room full of flowers, toys, and people, immersed in the golden light of silk-wrapped lamps.

Yet in the midst of this well-organized, good-natured freedom and naivety, intended to make light of the question of her youth and death, as opposed to her childish little sulks and whims, the truth known to everyone would swell in size, assume gigantic proportions.

Yes, her loyal friends came faithfully, always turning up in those brief hours between *repos complet*[59] and dinnertime.

Then they would vanish. And the pampered little girl, upon whom flowers and compliments had been generously lavished, would be left alone for the night with darkness and death.

22

Sometimes it transpired, however, that no one else was present and that she and I were alone, just the two of us. Then Mademoiselle Sossé would talk to me about matters closest to her heart. But she avoided sad topics with a peculiar wariness. I don't think she ever once complained.

Her memories of Armenia were mostly taken from books or perhaps from other people's stories. I had the impression that, to her, Armenia, her own country, was an *exotic* land. She informed me, for instance, that the Armenian Highland was once considered the highest place on earth because it was from there that the four great rivers of the world radiated: the Euphrates, the Araxes, the Gail, and the Chorokh.[60]

And after a while—without ceasing to smile—she added with a strange yearning expression:

"According to medieval tradition, that's where the earthly paradise is supposed to have been..."

Of her own exile, she spoke thus:

"It really was very unusual. As a child, before I came here, I lived for a time with a family I didn't know at all in a box in the municipal theater in Athens. I really did live in a theater box, I think for a few months."

She sifted with her slender fingers through a pile of papers kept in one of the folders and showed me an illustration cut from a newspaper—a photograph of an auditorium crammed with people and their belongings.

"Within that theater, the Athenians gave shelter to our exiles. Two thousand of us were accommodated there. In every one of the boxes a whole family lived, slept, and ate their meals. On the armrests, where Greek ladies once placed their sweet-boxes and opera-glasses, baskets of food and bundles of linen were hung, pillows lay piled up, laundry was drying. Inside every box, women cooked on makeshift stoves and fed their children. All the children were crying. And I cried too."

She was lost in thought for a moment.

"I can't remember what was on the stage, whether the curtain was down or not. Evidently I never looked in that direction…"

Again she broke off.

"And I had no idea then where Mama was…"

They rediscovered one another a few years later, but only by letter.

Mademoiselle Sossé sometimes spoke of her mother. But she never mentioned her father or the rest of her family.

In contrast to Mademoiselle Hovsepian and Monsieur Peynirian, who belonged to the Gregorian or Armenian Apostolic Church, Mademoiselle Sossé came from an Armenian-rite Catholic family.

She was very religious, bound to tradition, and well acquainted with all the intricacies and attractions of prayer.

She was very proud of the fact that in the year 301, long before other nations, the official state religion of Armenia had been Christianity. The Armenians paid for their loyalty to Christ's teaching with relentless wars against the Persians, because when the King of Kings insisted they restore the cult of Ahura Mazda, the Armenians rejected this demand. Armenia was also the only state in Asia to assist the Crusader knights with men and weapons. And various Popes expressed their gratitude for these services to Christianity.

In return for support, the Holy Roman Emperor Frederick Barbarossa later promised Prince Levon II the title of King. But since Barbarossa soon died, the title was conferred upon Levon by Emperor Henry VI, while Pope Celestine III sent one of his cardinals to attend the coronation.

Sossé always spoke in this way about her homeland, as though it were unfamiliar and lost in the mists of time, a fairy-tale land. She avoided thinking about the present, drawn only to what was past.

And that distant, exotic magic would flow over her and endow her frail, weak existence with a special kind of dignity.

She confessed to me once, shyly, modestly, as if it were highly embarrassing, that she sometimes tried to write. That she had attempted to translate Armenian songs.

When I pressed her, she read me a song in her singsong voice:

> *O sweet spring long ago,*
>> *Green time,*
> *You have vanished forever, forever.*
> *No more do I see the blue sky,*
> *Or hear the joyful song*
>> *Of small birds!*

> *You are gone, my beloved,*
> *Bearing away with you my happiness,*
> *Thus in vain the spring returns.*

> *Oh, the gay sun and laughing days*
> *Are gone, never to return,*
> *Thus in vain the spring returns.*

As soon as she'd finished reading, she said she was no longer interested in that kind of song and had translated it a long time ago.[61] But maybe I would like to hear how an old Armenian sings in exile:

> *All my dead are there,*
> *All those whom they killed…*

> *My children, children and grandchildren,*
> *Oh, my children, children and grandchildren.*

> *All my dead are there,*
> *All those whom they killed…*

She read it quickly, as if not wishing to delve into the substance of the words. Then she added:

"It's even by the old man who lost his mind, I think."[62]

Then she took out another piece of paper from the same folder and said: "Now I'll read you a prayer":

> Lord, have mercy upon us,
> Lord, have mercy upon us.
> Holy Trinity, send us peace on earth,
> Grant health to the sick!
> Console the suffering!
> Our Father, Our God, arise!
> Thou who art the refuge of the afflicted,
> Come to the aid of Thy servants
> And grant victory to the Christian armies.
> O, be Thou the refuge of the Armenian people!
> Lord, have mercy upon us![63]

"It's very beautiful," she asserted. "But only up to a point."

She showed me with her finger where the line "Console the suffering!" ended.

She did this so solemnly and with such deep significance, I was amazed.

"Why only up to there?"

"Because after that, there's a petition which God cannot answer."

Again I was amazed and urged her to explain.

"Why can't God grant you victory one day?"

Her little face grew sad from the strain. And eventually she said, with knitted brow and a forced expression on her lips:

"God cannot grant victory to one nation in its struggle against another. I don't believe one should ask for that, one ought not to…"

I still did not quite understand, so she concluded:

"I don't know—but it seems evident to me, that he *cannot*…"

23

At the charity bazaar in the Palace Hotel a number of ladies and gentlemen dressed up again in extraordinary costumes. But this time no one improvised, all the costumes were painstakingly thought out and realized.

The reception rooms of the *Jardin d'hiver* were completely transformed. A whole corner had been fenced off by a low railing and arranged with vases and pots of flowers in bloom. The scent of violets, hyacinths, lilacs, and lilies-of-the-valley gushed forth, while several ladies in Louis XV dresses sold bouquets or branches of the same flowers to anyone willing to buy them. Among the ladies sat Madame Saint-Albert in the same beautiful marchioness toilette as at our own Carnival party, looking once more like a young woman. As soon as she saw us, she began to beckon so we'd buy from her.

Around the room, beneath the palms, stood all manner of decorated kiosks, full of fantasy and illuminated by colored lights. But the most beautiful was the oriental tent where Turks in harmony with Arabs and Indians were handing out slightly cold Turkish coffee, and had hosts of objects for sale of no conceivable use to anyone. The interior of the tent was strewn with wondrously colored carpets. In the reddish semidarkness, ravishing oriental ladies sat on a huge sofa or lay on cushions scattered on the floor. Here Madame de Carfort had taken her place, dressed this time in the white costume of an Indian bayadère. Clearly she understood her own beauty and relished its type. We received from her the same black coffee, a little bottle made of yellow tin, a leather bookmark, and scores of colored glass bracelets that immediately shattered.

We threw balls at hideous mannequins that fell flat on their backs when hit on the head, won a single teacup and a single handkerchief, but absolutely nothing at all when we tried again later. We bought a tobacco pipe and then went into the dining room to rest from the excitement.

Here Madame Saint-Albert stood in wait in the passage, selling something else from a large basket. In addition to her husband and Carrizales, a group of other young men was standing around her.

Carrizales, as was his custom, was showering her with compliments, while holding under his arm a large doll he'd bought for Miss Norah and a box of writing-paper no one knew what for. And in his pocket he'd also concealed a large porcelain ink-pot.

Despite this he was determined to buy something extra from Madame Saint-Albert, whom he claimed today was a *horribile seductora*.

But then Mademoiselle Alice wafted past with some long, straight branches of white lilac in her arms. And, as she walked by, she flung a fleeting question toward the group of men.

They did not catch a word, but she merely laughed and refused to repeat it. And so eager to learn what it was, they all, except Saint-Albert and Carrizales, ran after her and did not return. After a while Carrizales too wandered off in that direction.

"Ten years more foolish than I, and ten years more fortunate," Madame Saint-Albert stated with a melancholy air.

Our circle of friends soon gathered around one table. Madame de Carfort in her white pearl-embroidered costume also joined us.

Customarily a woman of few words, she grew especially enlivened that evening. She spoke again of her Morocco, for which she was so homesick among the snows, and yet whose climate she could not tolerate. She had left behind a husband and son, and a garden full of flowers and palm trees, and her horse and dog—as well as her wonderful house—an old Arabian palace with its reception room partitioned off by a row of pillars—and quiet patio adorned in flowers.

She always kept a few photographs with her.

"Ah! How beautiful it is there. Beautiful and comfortable! *After what happened*, it would be difficult, impossible to live anywhere else."

On flimsy scraps of paper we looked at snapshots of magnificent countryside, hidden nooks of Moorish architecture, palm trees and sands, tiny alleys totally black in the blazing sun.

Of Madame de Carfort's wedding in a tiny church—so small because it'd been converted from an ordinary Arab house, as a monument to the terrible massacre of the French that had taken place there. And here was a photo of Madame de Carfort taken the day after her son was born—a dark figure lying propped against white bedding. And there she was again with her son— the same and yet different, like a Byzantine Madonna, her wonderful dark head bending over him.

"And that's Fatma," she said.

A dark-skinned young Arab woman posed gravely, holding the French child by the hand.

"She's his nanny. She idolizes him so much she'd give her life for him without a second thought. I can trust her completely, I am totally satisfied with her. She has only one fault, and that's that she's married. Because of that, we have a lot of problems."

Madame de Carfort laughed her gracious laugh. She was so animated and natural, so obviously moved by her reminiscences that only Monsieur Totsky might have listened to them reluctantly. Only Totsky—because Est was not there.

"But now everything is all right. They write from home that Fatma's husband has taken a second wife."

We didn't understand immediately.

"It was like this. Every few days the young Arab would appear at my house and ask solemnly and in all seriousness: 'Is it true that the evening before last you sent Fatma into town with a letter?' And I would reply, yes, it's true, I did send her.

"'Fatma didn't go into the kitchen to help the cook?'

"'No, she didn't.'

"'Will you allow Fatma to spend the night with me tonight?'

"'Yes, I will.'

"Reassured for a few days, Fatma's husband would ceremoniously say good-bye and depart.

"After every one of his visits Fatma was in despair. She would try to justify things and assured me it was not her fault. She really did everything she could to stop him talking to me.

"But he wouldn't give in. Her efforts only increased his suspicions. He was jealous and wouldn't believe any of her protestations until I had confirmed them.

"Fatma told me her husband wanted to take her back home.

"'But I shan't leave you,' she assured me. 'I keep telling him to take a second wife, that it'll be better that way. I shall always come to him whenever he wants—but he'll have the second wife and be calmer. She'll cook and bake for him, and I shall always be with the little one, and he won't keep running round and disturbing you.'

"'And you really won't regret it, if he obeys you and takes a second wife?' I asked. 'Because you do love him?'

"'Yes, I do love him, naturally. But I don't want him so suspicious of me all the time, don't want him to come here. It'll be far better when he has another wife.'

"And indeed, my husband now writes that he's become a better man since he took a second wife. And Fatma is now completely satisfied."

24

Mademoiselle Alice reappeared and at once made her way over to our table, of course, bringing in her wake Curchaud and Carrizales.

At the approach of Mademoiselle Alice, Madame de Carfort began to seethe. Since they were such hostile types, this was no surprise.

Her face stiffened, the smile froze on her lips, her eyes grew hard and lifeless, and words came out as if forced from her throat.

"She should not be tolerated. She's the type of woman who compromises women in general. She brings discredit on us all."

What can you say when someone feels like that? Ultimately, however, we were living in rarefied conditions up there in the mountains where no one is ever answerable for anything.

"Oh, I don't doubt she's not the only one amusing herself here with love affairs. Besides, I know nothing definite about her. But only she behaves like this toward men. And it's her way of carrying on—the level to which she sinks—that to me is unacceptable."

Madame de Carfort restrained herself for a moment, but was unable to prevent herself from saying it. And so she said it. Namely, that no young Frenchwoman, not even in that notorious Paris… And she knew herself what she said was naive.

I did not reply, but she sensed at once the lack of resonance between us and added hurriedly:

"Because you shouldn't draw conclusions from what they write in romances, where only French women are conclusively blackened."

How pretty and engaging she was in her desire for everything in her France to be perfect and without blemish. And she herself was the reason one had to believe her.

"And I know what's meant by truth in writing. Indeed I do," she added.

On this occasion too, as soon as Mademoiselle Alice appeared, Madame de Carfort assumed her customary look, supercilious and contemptuous. Mademoiselle Alice, however, was the only one who did not notice.

For Mademoiselle Alice simply *did not see* other women. She saw no one but herself, I would even say: *she was sufficient unto herself.* Her curiosity was exhausted and entirely satisfied by her own person.

"That de Carfort?" she would inquire absent-mindedly. "Is she pretty? No, I don't like her at all. She's not the type that appeals to men's tastes."

She interpreted Madame de Carfort's supercilious tone, taciturnity, and contempt quite otherwise:

"She's jealous, you can see it at once. How ridiculous. Does she really fancy that balding Curchaud? What do I do to make him follow me around all the time? I just make fun of him! But I'd gladly give him up, if she has such odd tastes. Though everybody's saying she's in love with that sick Jew, Est. Is it true?"

Madame de Carfort did indeed like talking to Monsieur Curchaud. She was so enthused by colonial affairs, by that whole exotic world drawn into the orbit of France's greatness. She herself—a flower of French expansionism in Africa—and Monsieur Curchaud—a planter from Cambodia—were as though the two outstretched arms of France embracing the southern and eastern extremities of the world: taken together, they were themselves an expression of the tremendous reach of French power.

Thus Madame de Carfort's face only brightened when she acquired Curchaud for a neighbor at the table and could talk again about what was closest to her heart. Mademoiselle Alice had seated herself at the far end between Monsieur Saint-Albert and Carrizales, who now "dared to gaze" into her amused eyes as if she'd never upbraided him for not respecting her.

"They understand what France brings them as a gift, they are beginning to understand," said Madame de Carfort. "We guaranteed them security in their own country, brought with us culture, railways, irrigation, law and order. We knew how to *win them over*... Now they are compliant, though always deeply steeped in their own traditions and faith, and in their pride, which is something I do admire in the Arabs. Do you know their biggest grudge against the French? That we gave the Jews the same rights, that Jews are now free to leave the ghetto..."

"It is possible to win them over, but only by strong military force," declared Carrizales stung by Madame de Carfort's words.

"Oh no, not only by force!" Madame de Carfort had many Arab friends, had proof not only of their submission but sympathy and gratitude. Among them she knew truly great lords who possessed an ancient culture and refined manners, and received colossal incomes from their land. She knew simple people like Fatma and her husband, as well as paupers resigned to their fate, who didn't understand it was possible to change it.

Neither she nor Carrizales could then have known that a few months later the Riffian rebellion, at that time struggling against Spain, would also turn against France.

"And then there's the story of our greatest enemy, El Amir Abd el-Kader, who fought us for many years. He died a genuine friend of the French."[64]

Mademoiselle Hovsepian, who might well have repeated at this point her naive outlook on world politics—"one nation should not oppress another"—was not among us that evening. Instead Monsieur Totsky, always in a contrary mood, was present.

"He died, but in prison." He unexpectedly qualified Madame de Carfort's words in his disagreeable voice.

"No, not in prison," Madame de Carfort replied as calmly as she could. "For six years he was indeed imprisoned, but then released. He died a free man. Or the activities of Father Foucauld![65] He too, through the sanctity of his life and great personal sacrifice, contributed to the victories of France, it wasn't just the army. For years he lived among different African tribes, one after another, and exerted such influence through his own example that those tribes later surrendered almost voluntarily, while others had to be captured by force."

"But the conclusion, the conclusion to this hagiographic idyll is highly instructive," Monsieur Totsky pressed his point. "Since he was murdered by the same blacks he'd inspired by his example."

Madame de Carfort's face clouded over and she heaved a sigh. But Monsieur Curchaud said it didn't mean anything, it was too bad: he died a hero.

"My own father, whom I can hardly remember, fell as an officer fighting in Senegal. Yet despite it my brother and I both settled in the colonies."

This time too Mademoiselle Alice turned her attention exclusively to Curchaud, ignoring her neighbors. Leaning across the table, she began to question him in a loud voice about his family, about Indochina, about Phnom Penh. As though she really wanted to know what it was like in Cambodia, actually like! After all, to her, who no longer had a homeland, it was a matter of total indifference. She could be here or elsewhere—yet everywhere a foreigner, far removed from home. Would Monsieur Curchaud, for example, be kind enough to take her with him—there, to Cambodia?

If she was thinking of settling somewhere for good, and remaining there till she died—then it was precisely there, in the heart of that wild and unknown land. So she would simply like to know when Monsieur Curchaud was leaving... But he was not to imagine it in his own way, get the wrong idea. Mademoiselle Alice would travel by herself as usual, and ask him only for a little care and protection.

Monsieur Curchaud imagined it only that way too, naturally. Everything seemed to suggest nevertheless that her conditions conformed admirably with his own desires and yet continued to expose her to the same dangers and anxieties without which she simply could not live.

Madame de Carfort was the first to rise from the table. What a contrast to that crowded, colorful evening to find ourselves once more amid the dark night strewn with snow and stars!

We returned on foot taking the shortcut across the park and down the steep paths and stairways built of stones or hewn from the rock. The electric lamps froze and receded in the snow-covered thickets. It was pure delight to breathe the black frosty air.

Monsieur Totsky walked beside me and spoke of what was most important to him:

"She understands everything, she's sensitive, subtle, intelligent. But French reasons of state—they are the threshold. And Madame de Carfort does not know how to cross that threshold. She may, like Carrizales, resent the fact that the Arabs want independence. She may, like Curchaud, consider opium to be harmless because it helps balance the state budget…"

In the flickering lights I could see his face and ugly grimace, which expressed the genuine torture of his heart. He clenched and unclenched his fingers to no purpose as he spoke, and even cracked his joints like simple people do.

"Those Arabs there, their homes, their country—what are they to her, even to her who likes them…? And the imprisonment of Abd el-Kader and the death of that missionary—what of this comprises any part of her own beautiful life there for which she is so homesick—her Arabian house, her palm-tree garden, even her car and horse…?"

Monsieur Totsky was in love with Madame de Carfort, but could not accept her as she was. That's how it sometimes is between people. And who knows whether it's not the worst form of unhappy love.

25

Miss Norah called from her balcony each morning that it was beautiful weather and spring had arrived. But from below, Carrizales would laugh and protest, not yet.

To this day, I cannot say exactly when spring did arrive. In one place it seemed to be definitely there—whereas in another, very close place, there was no sign of it at all. A shadow cast by the forest, a bend in the rock-face was enough to dispel illusions at once.

For weeks on end we lived disorientated. Every outing, every walk was simply a meandering through time.

One warm sunny day we descended five kilometers along the main road through wet snow into a delightful secluded valley, not visible from our villa.

The world was simply transformed before our eyes. Bare trees were already bursting with swollen buds. In pastures still awash with melted snow the strange village women, clad in black woolen dresses and black straw hats, were spreading manure over the grass. In these costumes, they looked like provincial ladies paying visits in their Sunday best or walking to high mass.

The road gradually changed into a charming avenue lined by very old, low stone walls. On either side we could smell ivy, myrtle, and box.

At one point on the road, the steep mountainside was underpinned by an old stone wall, but above it, higher up the slope, a still bare deciduous grove was growing, warmed by the sun, interspersed by an undergrowth of evergreen bushes. The pungent, slightly bitter fragrance of southern leaves came rushing toward us like a hot sultry breeze on a summer's day.

The electric railway took us farther afield, up again into the high mountains, into an empty snowy world of towering peaks, forests, and precipices. From there we rode even farther away— along a wonderful soaring track, dashing as if through the air along high ledges and over bridges above deep chasms. From the window we could see the slender green stream of the Grande Eau flowing directly beneath us in the deep narrow floor of the canyon. Just peering down inspired fear mingled with delight.

At a given moment the steep opposite rim of the gorge fell away and revealed a distant wall of mountains touching the sky and fencing in a vast expanse of valleys, mountains and ridges. And there high up, high above, resting on the very crest of the wall, amid the vertically ascending snow-bedecked forests, we caught a fleeting glimpse of our settlement—a handful of tiny white boxes glued to the snow. It dominated the whole surrounding world from above, nothing could be seen beyond it but the sky. Then, like a hallucination, it disappeared from view behind a bend in the track, which rearranged yet again the entire configuration of ridges, slopes, and chasms.

It was hard to believe that our home, our room, our balcony with the choucas was there—that we were actually there, in the midst of that world.

Then we were descending from our flight under the sky, nestling close to the mountainside, dashing over bridges and stone buttresses, through tunnels, circling ever lower and lower—until we reached the wide green valley of the Rhône. The world grew more intimate, tangible, commonplace, and for a moment all was obscured by the seemingly massive bulk of the little railway station.

We left behind us the few old streets of the small town and came in the late afternoon to the Rhône, along a straight, level, wide white road. The mountains stood far off—pink and violet in the sunset haze. They had shifted to the distant edge of the horizon, like a tantalizing mirage. We walked between flat meadows and orchards, now turning green like those at home, among the damp warm fragrances of the earth, among bird calls—and we were suddenly transported into the heart of spring, as if a magic spell had been cast upon us.

We returned home from our first excursion into spring by night—in falling snow, darkness, and freezing temperatures.

But the days went by. Already, where we lived, the sun-facing slopes were running with melted snow. The first flowers emerged into the air from the yellow grass of the meadows: lemon-colored primroses, sapphire gentians, and stiff, naive, indifferent, white or violet crocuses. And between the colored flowers, the grass grew greener every day.

The chaffinches, who had pre-empted events earlier on, were now definitely right. Their cheerful, persistent, resolute song reverberated through the forest merging into the joyful chorus of other spring birds.

But still it was enough to climb only a very short distance up the mountain for the bald patches of melting snow on the grass, or yellow pastures with their first flowers, to suddenly disappear. We stepped again into a world of severe winter—the crunch of deep, frost-encrusted snow beneath our feet—into forests of giant spruce still shedding remnants of former snowfalls, in among

83

steep magical crags, whole walls of flaky pink rock. Chunks of ice floated in the stone drinking-troughs placed at intervals along the road for the cows that came in summer.

At bends in the road, in gaps between the huge trees, ever new windows opened onto the vast vista of the world. But nothing appeared green from there, and the Rhône valley was not visible at all.

After a hazy day, a fine evening would follow. The sun would set in a blaze of glorious color. The enormous basin of slopes and valleys would fill with milky blue darkness while the white summits turned pink above streaks of cloud as though traced in the air.

A light frost would take hold as darkness fell. Yet at the same time, in the valley below, the warm earth would be exuding its scents and the lilac veils of twilight enveloping the first green leaves.

26

When Monsieur Est said on one occasion that the whole League of Nations had taken its seat at our table, he was not only correct but somehow anticipating events.[66]

For we also had a German, our very own German, as I mentioned before, and the most authentic kind of German, because from Berlin. Like many other Germans, he too was called Fuchs.

He would sit down to eat with us and sometimes even express his views. We were united in our dislike—we all spoke of him, as a German, with malice and antipathy. Monsieur Verdy could not refer to him except as "that swine Fuchs," or "that blackguard Fuchs." But his blunt talk offended not only Madame de Carfort.

The rest of us were more restrained. We considered it possible to exchange a few pleasantries with him, and no one caused him any direct offence.

In spite of this, he must have sensed perfectly that he was entirely alone. He was on one side of the fence and we were all on the other—separated from him.

He must have felt it—but gave nothing away. He was even sure of himself, rather free and independently minded.

He seemed to treat everything with a touch of irony, a little perversely and not entirely seriously. He always smiled first, and only then began to speak. And this strange, false "putting on a good face" also made an uncomfortable impression.

Since the end of the war, for several years, he had undergone constant treatment. He had been round all the sanatoria in his own country and now come to us, as if making a final bid.

Yet he was not seriously ill. He looked well and had very red, unpleasantly thick lips. He was able to take walks, converse, go on excursions. But no one was interested in what he really lacked or needed.

Indeed, no one knew what weighed on his soul—behind that bitter, ironic little smile—and no one was keen to find out.

With the sole exception of Madame Wogdeman.

He stood outside the doors of life—beyond friendship, beyond the sweet nectar of understanding.

Even Mademoiselle Alice, generally so indulgent, so—how can I put it?—undiscriminating, never regarded him as a potential danger.

On one particular occasion Monsieur Totsky was making malicious jokes about the war. No one was surprised. Everyone knew he took pride in the neutrality of his adoptive country.

Fuchs listened and turned bright red, pulling pained faces and biting his too crimson, too full lips.

At last he said:

"As soon as I recover, I shall return immediately to the army. Yes, I know they'll take me—so long as I recover…"

Monsieur Verdy glanced at Fuchs with a distasteful expression on his face and inquired:

"So you wish to go on fighting?"

We turned to Fuchs. No, he did not look warlike. He couldn't really be thinking of revenge, all on his own. He was too weak, too tired, somehow too unhappy.

"You still want to fight?" Monsieur Verdy was irritated. "Well that is remarkable! Today when the whole world desires peace! Haven't you had enough of war and its consequences?"

Everyone sensed we ought not to discuss it here, now. But Monsieur Verdy was not the most tactful of men. Fuchs proved not to be tactful either.

"It's easy to be a pacifist *now*," he said after a long silence, and his ironic smile looked like a wry contortion. "Before you relieved us of Alsace and Lorraine, you deemed every pacifist in France to be a traitor."

We were all of the opinion such a conversation was out of place and remained silent in our disapproval. Perhaps Monsieur Verdy would have wished to say something further, but Madame de Carfort intervened and prevented him. With an expression of anger and abhorrence, she rose from her seat and asked Monsieur Verdy for a quiet word. It transpired it was something relatively unimportant, namely newspapers for the sick Est.

Herr Fuchs received no response whatsoever to his statement. Ultimately, no one was curious either about Fuchs's affairs or his opinions.

No one, that is, except Madame Wogdeman, who was absent moreover at that moment; Madame Wogdeman—the one with the eyes that always stared the farthest, as far away as possible.

I once encountered her in the room of Miss Norah, to whom I paid a neighborly visit, bringing a glass of her favorite wine.

On the balcony, where Norah lay naked as usual, there again stood a vase of roses. Now I knew who they were from and what they signified.

She lay on her stomach with her back exposed, beautiful and bronzed, baked by the hot sun, glowing like molten metal.

Her elbows were propped on the embroidered pillow, her head held in the soft shade of the roses.

She put down her book and drank the wine, laughing and re-joicing at something—like Mary Magdalene bent over her Bible unrepentant, or simply a bacchante.

She asked how we'd enjoyed ourselves at the charity bazaar, and who we'd been on excursions with. She already knew it all anyway, since she'd been told by the Vigils—by Mr and Mrs Vigil, and also by Señor Carrizales, whom she understood better and better now, because she was still learning Spanish.

She was carefree, joyful, untouched by the tortures of anxiety or suspicion, immune to the fantastical imaginings of jealousy. It was enough that he came to tell her how he'd been enjoying himself elsewhere.

I remembered this same Carrizales at the charity bazaar and on our walks, remembered what he'd said to Madame Saint-Albert and what Mademoiselle Alice had said about him.

But Miss Norah was always there—immobile and expectant, fixed to the place like a plant that had taken root.

And when I thought about him and about her, and that they were like the butterfly and the rose, there was far more truth in the comparison than there usually was.

But that wasn't what I wanted to discuss. Rather the arrival of Madame Wogdeman. First we talked about our Armenian friends, and then about Fuchs.

"Yes, you told me," Miss Norah cried at once. "I feel terribly sorry for him…"

I was surprised at the sympathy both women showed for Fuchs, who did not look at all depressed and wasn't even par-ticularly ill. And who was only too ready to go on fighting…

Madame Wogdeman spoke strangely in her soft breathless voice.

"What can those, for whom the war brought victory, or libera-tion, possibly know about it? When they carried off from that abyss *a sense of gratified moral righteousness*—the unmistakable trophy, the talisman promising solace and balsam to all their wounds…?"

She spoke in such a solemn manner, I was taken aback.

From her I learned that Fuchs's lung had been shot through twice during the war and that he was unable to regain his strength, to fully recover, after suffering major blood loss.

"But the gravest wound, and for him a mortal one, is surely his wounded pride, his eternally humiliated *amour propre*… His wounds remain forever open and so he can never be healthy."

"Yes," said Miss Norah. "He is almost as unfortunate as little Sossé, who is also unable to recover."

Madame Wogdeman shook her head as she stared over Norah's naked body and into the far distance at the furthermost snowcapped peak rearing into the sky.

"No, no, Mademoiselle Sossé is not so unfortunate. The Armenians have kept the self-esteem of those who suffered innocently. Everything noble in Europe and America sympathizes with their agony. But this Fuchs—who still wants revenge, retaliation—can he keep referring, morally, to the injuries done to him? When everyone knows, when he must know himself—when he has no illusions…? And yet he too fought then, like others—and also suffered…"

She broke off for a moment to take breath. A remarkable thing, but each breath was more like a sigh.

"When I look at him, it seems to me he's been alive too long, outlived his own death by a few years. It's not such a rare phenomenon. Outlived his own death in order to experience it better, more thoroughly. He feels he already knows it by heart—to the very last breath. How arduous must be the moral effort of the conquered—the *rightfully* conquered[67]—to somehow motivate themselves psychologically, come to terms with things, find a way out—if only to help themselves, if only to spite everyone else…

"Moral strength provides a way out of the most grievous injury. But Fuchs has no way out. His agony is a fruitless wrestling with the truth of defeat, without deliverance and without justification."

"You think that's how he feels?"

"I think that's how he feels. And so he seems to me more dead than Mademoiselle Sossé or that poor Est dying by turns between joking and despair…"

27

How we were drawn to the valleys at that time, despite the beauty of the summits!

Snow fell again in the mornings, only to melt an hour later. A warm sun would emerge from white mist dripping with light.

Everywhere was white, like in winter. Thus we decided, with the Saint-Alberts, to walk down to the Rhône plain by the shortest route along a precipitous footpath and have breakfast in the nearest little town.

This time our walk became a veritable ramble through several climatic zones.

First, we walked over snow in the chill shade of ancient spruce, between hard, solid walls of rock. But the snow came to an end along with the forest, and we were greeted by steep slopes of pastureland, in some places already genuinely green, arrayed with brilliantly colored flowers. The rocky path, strewn with loose stones, scrunching and grinding beneath our feet, twisted and turned, and skirted now a bulge in the slanting meadow, now a remnant of the spruce forest. Sometimes, as it clung to a ledge on the rose-grey rockface, the path would hang over a ravine where green water roared far below. Other times, flanked by two lines of bare bushes, it would drop down so violently it felt as if it too would end in a precipitous cliff, a dozen or so feet from where we were. Eventually it led, tunnel-like, into a thick, dense, still-denuded deciduous forest and went on like that for a long time. Here and there leafless branches sprang out of green trunks, coiled with ivy as far as the tree-tops.

Every step was a perpetual battle with the steepness of the path. Stepping forward meant constantly resisting the impulse to run. Grating little stones overtook us and scuttled away below. Boulders lay on either side, creating whole slopes and walls amid the dense leafless forest as it plunged down the mountainside along with the path, with ourselves—and with truly alarming speed.

Every opening in the trees or rocks revealed the same unchanging outline of the Dents du Midi, blown like glass out of silver. And yet the view was constantly changing. The mountains farthest away grew smaller and smaller as if setting behind the nearer ones, which in turn were thrust upwards—sometimes almost touching the sky. Each time the mountain world grew less magnificent and less extensive, framed by less and less imposing chasms of empty air. And each time the loveliness of the valley drew closer and appeared more real.

After we'd been descending for an hour and a half, the celebration of genuine spring began in earnest. Clumps of trees stood in green clearings sprinkled with the golden down of young leaves. Roundish, emerald-green gooseberry bushes marked the pathways to cottages. Trees in the narrow lanes blossomed pink and white, while the tall grass in the orchards shone with a deep, warm malachite-green.

Madame Saint-Albert and I walked side by side without uttering a word. Our eyes strayed far into the distance, into fathomless depths of air and light. The earth was too beautiful. It seemed to be summoning us toward something—and placing us under some kind of obligation. It wasn't easy to respond to such a call.

My acquaintance with Madame Saint-Albert had reached the stage where we each felt the need and prospect of knowing the truth about the other.

I don't recall having asked her anything particular, or having intentionally hastened the moment of candor that was fast approaching. But it came nevertheless.

"Earlier in life, when I was happy," said Madame Saint-Albert, "I always imagined I would know how to grow old. I felt a composure within me and an acceptance of life's course—I was equal to it. I was already flaunting my youth when I was fifteen years old. But only now do I understand that youth is not a state. It is a value added to everything, it imparts reality to life. And old age is the removal of value from everything, from the least thing."

She spoke slowly, with effort, searching for words.

I looked at her and sensed there wasn't anything I could say, not even about the natural world all around us, from which my eyes were swimming in intoxication.

She replied to the words I had not uttered.

"I do not see the beauty of the world. I try to free myself from it, though it pursues me like an animal, fawns on me. Whether it's up there on the mountain or down here, I am alone in relation to it, alien, blind. I look at everything around me as if at something that's come after me. Terrible loneliness, vast emptiness…"

I no longer recall how it sounded coming from my lips, but I probably said something about him, reminded her almost harshly that she was loved. After all, her words were unjust to his young feelings, which were obvious to everyone.

She was silent for a moment. Then she said severely:

"He's too distant from me. He hangs over me but can do nothing for me. He's powerless."

I was not watching her at that moment.

"His youth torments and hurts me. How can I turn to him, even notice him? How can I live through my own separate, private affair along with him, with him by my side? I don't see him at all because of this terrible thing. I have to concentrate, get to the bottom of it, muster my strength somehow in order to, in order to be able to…"

We came to a halt. Here the footpath dived into a sudden bend and came out lower down the mountainside between two stone enclosure walls. Hot air blew out from there as from an electric hairdrier.

Immediately below this verdant spring, a noontide of scorched limestone began. The entire bare slope facing the sun was criss-crossed by a network of stone-walled enclosures and regular stone staircases. The vineyards confined within these small rectangles—scarcely bigger sometimes than what looked like the size of a pocket handkerchief—were still almost naked, yet regularly dotted with the tiny points of vine-shoots close to the ground, bristling with hundreds of evenly spaced stakes, cleanly dug and meticulously tidied. They gave the impression across the whole landscape, of a gigantic, painstaking, and sumptuous piece of embroidery, realized solely for the sake of embellish-ment. The vertical spires of cypresses rose up here and there. Huge trees covered in pink blossom hung over stone cottages.

We walked on further without looking at each other. Now I wished her to be silent. Perhaps she wished it too. But at a par-ticular moment she added:

"I am drowning, drowning. But he is on the bank and must remain on the bank—he can't rescue me even though he longs to. He can do nothing for me..."

I turned my head towards her. And then I saw.

The years swept over her before my very eyes. As she spoke, her face grew dark from despair. Blackened, aged, from her very words. The creases around her mouth, when she eventually shut it tight, hardened into black furrows.

Beyond the next twist in the path the Rhône valley sparkled before us at last like a huge emerald set in its mount of hillsides, framed by walls, vineyards, and cypresses, as luxurious as Para-dise—so close, it seemed within a hand's grasp above the low stone wall.

Crossed by white roads, embroidered by little towns, each with its old castle or convent, festooned by flowering gardens—it was a delight to the eyes, the longed-for haven for the weary of wandering.

Our path led down between vineyards onto the bright street of a little town. The stone houses had shutters made of green wooden slats. The scent of myrtle, box, and laurel wafted from gardens. Buds of flowering climbers, which grew everywhere out of cracks in the stone, clung to the walls like little balls of violet and gold.

Now we were all walking together, our legs wobbling at the knees, summoning what energy still remained to find somewhere to rest. At last we sat down at a table in the garden of a hotel, surrounded by bare plane-trees with their dappled bark and lopped-off branches—looking like giant candelabra.

Monsieur Saint-Albert, delighted by the expedition, looked into his wife's eyes with joy and happiness. He'd been thinking we absolutely must fly *par avion* over the lake to Geneva. It had to be, since he desired it so much. While she, seduced by the momentum of his words and charm of his smile, eventually smiled herself—with great effort and anguish.

While I thought to myself: that unmentionable thing—growing old—is that bad...? That imminent and inevitable thing, against which nothing can protect us except death, that imminent and implacable thing—is it really so terrible?[68]

28

Every day after dinner Madame de Carfort spent half an hour with poor Est, confined now to his bed. But she never went alone. She was usually accompanied by the older, serious, and very shy Lady Malden.

She confessed to me that her visits were the boy's only pleasure. So she couldn't refuse him.

"Things are very bad with him and none of his close family is here. He's homesick for his Romania and dreams of dying there—absolutely there, and not here. But I don't think he could travel in his condition..."

The last few days had been worse. Doctors from outside had been called in and Est's father was to be summoned by telegram. Madame de Carfort was deeply affected by it, almost transformed.

That day she'd wanted to visit him as usual, but Lady Malden had already left for good. She asked if we'd like to accompany her this time. Naturally, we agreed at once.

He smiled when we entered. His ugly, mournful face lit up. That charming woman was his last joy.

He listened cheerfully as she chided him for his low spirits and disobedience toward Sister and the doctors. She claimed these were just whims, mere caprices, and that he should now lie calmly, and his temperature would drop.

He seemed to believe her a little, lulled by her words. But he alone believed. *It* is always immediately obvious once it begins to draw near—in the facial expression, in the hard-to-define change in the smile. Est had always been pale and thin, though, and never ceased to *faire de l'esprit*,[69] even now.

"My God, how many Jews there are in the world," he enthused. "And no one likes them anywhere. I was simply thrown out of Romania. Everywhere, generally speaking, they want to get rid of us. When I recover I must address the matter seriously. Assemble all Jews capable of bearing arms in one place. Not in Palestine, God forbid, there are too many amateurs there. I'll have to think, where. And we'll invade Europe. All those not in favor will be exterminated and we'll found a Jewish state. Of course it'll be a monarchy. And as a reward for my services I'll be elected king."

Madame de Carfort listened with a friendly smile—anxious only that Est was talking too much.

"Those are my most immediate projects," Est went on. "Do you think I'd lay my cards on the table, if I didn't stand a chance? Now, I have to leave a lot of things unsaid. But if I were king of the Jews, it would give me self-confidence—wouldn't it? And then I would ask for your hand. Is it so easy to refuse the hand of a king?—even if he's king of the Jews?"

Madame de Carfort reminded him she was not free to dispose of her hand.

"Well, what of it?" said Est. "Monsieur de Carfort would be sentenced to life imprisonment or even death. Such impediments can't be taken seriously."[70]

He stared at her—weak, dying, and yet amused by this, his final game.

"You can't condemn my intentions, you who are a monarchist…"

This time Est's jokes were certainly foolish, and yet they did not offend the fastidious Madame de Carfort. Everything was forgiven since he was about to die.

Then we listened to the soft music of a little gramophone that Est could no longer set in motion himself, and no longer accompany with his jazz. Then we looked through some books— the strange, exquisite novels of Panaït Istrati, of whom Est was so proud.[71]

As we prepared to leave, his mood changed.

"So what?" he said gloomily with the sad grimace of an ugly child. "You'll go back to your Africa and be happy. But I…"

I watched Madame de Carfort, always so inaccessible and severe and simply unable to abide Totsky, who was just as unhappily in love with her as Est. Now her smile was full of tenderness and her eyes misted over with tears.

Yes. For Est's love was full of grace, and Totsky's completely devoid of it.

29

Of late we had seen less of Madame de Carfort.

The spring sunshine had enticed us out to perpetual wandering, high into the mountains or down into the valley. I knew Madame de Carfort's prejudices, so it was difficult to invite her when we were accompanied by Mademoiselle Alice. And Mademoiselle Alice always wanted to go everywhere, heard about everything before anyone else, looked forward to it, and jumped for joy at any proposal. Mademoiselle Alice attached herself to us more often than not, thereby excluding Madame de Carfort, who showed less initiative.

Besides, Madame de Carfort was not in a sociable mood just then. I had the impression she was genuinely worried about Est's steadily worsening condition and devoting more time to him than before.

On the other hand, Madame Saint-Albert, herself so frigid and austere, saw nothing reprehensible in the behavior of Mademoiselle Alice. In contrast to Madame de Carfort, she was much more tolerant of other people.

"It's entirely natural considering her youth," she once said of Alice to Madame de Carfort. "She's so pretty and charming it doesn't offend me at all."

Yes. She was not offended at all by that very same youth in Mademoiselle Alice which she was unable to forgive in her husband.

I recall one particular walk when her tolerance was put to the test, so to speak. A walk in which Mademoiselle Alice participated.

We were to walk only a short distance down the mountain to the nearest village and return home for breakfast by car.

Mademoiselle Alice, walking ahead with Monsieur Curchaud, suddenly summoned Monsieur Saint-Albert to her side. Allegedly, she wanted to get down the mountain faster in order to find a drink of water, because she was thirsty. Did Monsieur Saint-Albert not know a quicker route…?

Having thus safeguarded the rear (because we were walking immediately behind them along with Monsieur Totsky and Monsieur de Flèche), she began to jest with her companion without constraint. In order to spite Curchaud, she took Saint-Albert's arm when crossing steeper sections of the path, and made him pick the violet crocuses and lemon-colored primroses growing in more dangerous places, throwing them away afterwards when they got in her way.

My thoughts were still strongly affected by Madame Saint-Albert's recent confidences, although nothing more had been said since that earlier outing. Perhaps she would have preferred me not to have remembered so precisely. But I could no longer fail to see the intense, ever-present, never-ending anguish behind the cold mask of her face.

I remember how nothing of that spring—those meadows, flowers, the emerald-green spread of the valley, the peach trees blossoming down below—none of it gave her any joy.

"I am not going to flirt with your husband," Mademoiselle Alice cried out to her, turning round. "Never fear! I really do have a great liking for him, but only as a sister!"

The words were out—or, one might say, the challenge was out. And I believe we were all then mindful of only one thing. No one glanced at Madame Saint-Albert. The provocative nature of Alice's words, her cry and laughter, was all too obvious and—albeit artless and meaningless—in this instance inappropriate.

Perhaps only Monsieur Saint-Albert was not offended by them, since he replied gaily:

"Well, too bad. I'll have to be satisfied with that!"

He answered her with a joke—glibly, aptly, in a similar tone of voice, on the same level. He took up the challenge. And we all took note of that too.

Everyone could see there was no comparison between the bold, brazen insolence of youth and the composure of the faded older woman. Monsieur Saint-Albert surely did not make such comparisons—he was too considerate for that and too kind. But perhaps it was worse he no longer compared.

On Madame Saint-Albert's side there was his love, no one doubted that. But everything else was on Mademoiselle Alice's. And for the time being, maybe only for the duration of that walk, it was too late to rescue anything; there was nothing to be said.

At first Monsieur Curchaud continued to walk with them, tagging along with all the deftness of his forty-year-old sportsman's legs. He too climbed up to reach out-of-the-way flowers, he too had something to say from time to time, he too wiped the sweat from his receding brow. But at a given moment he fell behind, which the other two didn't even notice in their laughing, flower-filled, reckless descent.

The full light, warmth, and spring had restored the values of the world to their natural, rightful place.

One might agree with Madame de Carfort that Mademoiselle Alice was undiscriminating, her coquetry unsavory, her methods of attracting men too unceremonious. Well, yes. But whatever means she employed—her goal was always one and the same, in harmony with nature, with the spring and its beauty.

The day after this excursion Mademoiselle Alice discovered me in the reading room before dinner and, taking advantage of our being alone, shared the things that were troubling her.

"You won't believe what I went through yesterday with that Curchaud! He's convinced I'll agree to become his wife and go with him to Asia. However did he get that into his head? Men really are ridiculous! He made such a scene because of his jealousy over Saint-Albert. What an idea! What do I care about Saint-Albert? I threatened that if he didn't cease at once, I would stop the car and return home on foot."

She was silent for a moment and then smiled.

"But this Saint-Albert really does make me wonder. You remember how I compelled him not to pester me, not to show me any attention. Whereas yesterday you saw for yourself, didn't you? He simply couldn't leave me alone, the whole way. I feel terrible about it—because of her. Given his temperament, she must be an awfully unhappy woman."

Mademoiselle Alice became thoughtful.

"You were talking a long time yesterday to Monsieur de Flèche," she remarked with great solemnity. "What do you make of him? He certainly is an interesting, profound man, at least he gives that impression. Why doesn't he leave, since the doctors have given their permission, since he's completely cured? He seems oddly cold and indifferent. Could it be possible he's fallen in love with that sick Armenian, Mademoiselle Sossé? I find it hard to believe…"

Mademoiselle Alice's questions were rather rhetorical, for she seemed not to wait for my answers—but to work things out for herself in a way that best suited her.

"But one thing Saint-Albert cannot refuse me," she suddenly declared emphatically. "Tomorrow I must speak with him for half an hour in private, alone. After what happened yesterday, I have no idea what he's thinking, what he's after, what he's banking on in relation to me…"

She talked of her complicated and disturbing affairs for quite some time, impassioned and inflamed. At last she stood up. She had remembered that from six o'clock Monsieur Curchaud would be waiting for her in the tea room and would again make a scene, suspecting her of God knows what.

30

One evening, in Mademoiselle Sossé's room, I finally found out who Madame Wogdeman was—that elusive taciturn lady with ashen face and eyes fixed on the far distance.

Monsieur Totsky was speaking of things which keenly interested the little Armenian. He believed in the possibility of war never happening again. Believed a time would come when there would be no more wars, believed they were not necessary. And he saw indications of this in modern religious thought aimed at pacifying the world.

In his awkward, somewhat caustic manner he expounded the next installment of what Fuchs had previously interrupted.

This time Fuchs was absent, so there was no threat to our discussion from that quarter. The very presence of Madame de Carfort, however, had to be taken into consideration.

"The most important thing going on at the moment," stated Totsky, without avoiding Madame de Carfort's gaze, "is the process thinkers have called the 'internationalization of God.'"

"Yes," he insisted, although Madame de Carfort hadn't uttered a word. "It's a matter of momentous importance though not everybody sees it. Because this is something demonstrated by Switzerland, a country that has its prophets even today—men who have rejected their chairs in theology to live in working-class districts and proclaim the imminent coming to earth of the Kingdom of God. In other words, it has proved possible—for the sake of realizing a particular, defined conception of social, and hence moral, existence—to reconcile and unite what may seem impossible to reconcile anywhere else: languages, races and religions, not simply different ones, but those that are actually opposed to one another, or even hostile. This unusual model—of creating a strong nation out of hybrid humanity—is a lesson to the world in how to create humanity out of warring nations."

For a moment no one spoke. A remarkable thing: all the foreigners there in Switzerland—traveling from different parts of the world, the sons and daughters of great nations—assumed a tone of almost making light, almost jocular approval of this country of whose culture, hospitality, and beauty they so readily availed themselves. As if they still thought like Victor Hugo that *"La Suisse trait sa vache et vit paisiblement…"*[72]

No one responded to Monsieur Totsky's words. But no one responded, it seemed, merely out of politeness. After a pause Madame de Carfort ventured to say something:

"And what's that supposed to mean: the 'internationalization of God'?"

Monsieur Totsky eagerly took up the cue:

"It's quite clear. Just remind yourself, please, what wars were like in ancient times. Assyria waged war in the name of its god, Assura, whose authority came to an end where the territory of his state came to end. The polytheism of our ancestors was a constant, never-ending dispute between warring gods. In antiquity, every tin-pot country had its own god, whose protection and participation it would invoke—its own 'lord of hosts.' And all wars to date, all over the world, go on trying to involve heaven, militarize God, demand He should descend into the earth's mud and blood. Before going into battle they pray for victory, for the engagement of heavenly forces, for *intervention.*—What's this, if not a hangover from polytheism?"

Little Sossé lay quietly in her bed among her flowers and playthings, and listened with childish concentration, a straight little furrow visible between her eyebrows. But her eyes constantly made their way back to the face of Monsieur de Flèche—as if she wished to learn the truth of what Totsky said only from what she saw written there.

It was evident that Monsieur de Flèche listened to Totsky's words under duress. When there was a lull in the conversation, he began to speak slowly, with deliberation:

"The life of the recently canonized Thérèse of the Child Jesus contains the testimony of a woman whom she restored to health, one Marie Duereux.[73] Once when Marie was engrossed in prayer imploring God to grant victory to the French, Saint Thérèse appeared to her and said: '*It is not permitted to penetrate the decrees of God*.'"

Sossé did not now take her eyes off the speaking man.

"This is the truth that people have to understand: that God is *above the nations.* They have to understand that they cannot pray for everything, that they are not free to pray for anything…"

Sossé smiled involuntarily at Monsieur de Flèche even though he was not looking at her, feeding on his every word.

She trusted him as she relived yet again that great sacrifice, investing all her hope in the unquestionable truth of his words.

Monsieur Totsky interrupted:

"France was the first to overcome the shocking blindness of centuries. Her armies went into battle without praying for victory. And there will come a time when all nations will comprehend God's neutrality. His internationalization will ensue. And then war will become impossible, having lost its sanction."

Now Madame de Carfort spoke up:

"That's not true. What you're referring to are the ideas of Wilfred Monod, who is not a Catholic. He also reminds me of your 'liberated' Swiss prophet Leonhard Ragaz, who instructs the Zurich workers in I know not what.[74] And I know not how he imagines the Kingdom of God on earth—I suspect not unlike the Republic of Soviets."

As she spoke, Monsieur Totsky's face clouded over. The light in his eyes simply faded and went out.

"But one thing I do know for sure," Madame de Carfort went on, "that no great cause in the history of the world ever triumphed without bloodshed."

"Even Christianity," Monsieur Totsky muttered under his breath without looking at her.

"Yes, even Christianity," she reiterated calmly.

31

Throughout this conversation I sat in a corner of Mademoiselle Sossé's flowery room on a soft small sofa next to Madame Wogdeman, who likewise remained silent.

At the point where Madame de Carfort in her excitement mentioned the Republic of Soviets, I felt Madame Wogdeman flinch uneasily.

I vaguely knew she'd been through some grave ordeals in her own country, experienced things she couldn't talk about. There are so many of those Russian princesses loose in the world, abounding in French novels and theatrical productions, whose husbands had been killed or diamonds requisitioned, poetic ladies, rich aristocrats who'd been reduced to beggars—their plight is familiar enough. I imagined something of the kind in the case of Madame Wogdeman and had no difficulty being discreet in my relationship with her.

The same thing occurred, however, as recently with Madame Saint-Albert. Madame Wogdeman also desired to tell me the truth about herself. It was totally different from what I'd expected.

"I am not an émigrée out of necessity, you know?" she announced in her soft, breathless voice. "I could go back there…"

"Is that so?" I said in anticipation.

"Yes. I could return at any time if I wanted."

She took a deep breath, in a way that made it sound like a sigh.

"But I am not going back," she concluded and sighed again.

I imagined that was all and listened further to the conversation of the others.

But Madame Wogdeman leant her ashen face closer to me and said almost silently:

"I myself don't want to return. Do you understand? Wogdeman … is my maiden name. In fact, my name is N…"

"Is that so?" I inquired again.

"Yes. N… He is actually my husband."

A slight whiff of drama accompanied this revelation prompting a degree of distrust but, at the same time, curiosity to know more.

"So I could return, since my husband is part of the government, *n'est-ce pas*?"

I replied as impartially as I could.

"I daresay he does it out of conviction…"

"Oh yes," she replied hastily.[75] "He is deeply convinced that the cause is good. I know that for sure. There is no sacrifice he wouldn't hesitate to make… I was there. I was there by his side from the very first day and saw everything, the armed struggle and the blood…"

It was precisely at this point that Madame de Carfort had addressed her words to Totsky: "no great cause in the history of the world ever triumphed without bloodshed."

Madame Wogdeman was silent for a while listening. But then she began again:

"Yes. Because what was there before was wrong and had to perish. The anger of the common people was just. The war was wrong, and the imprisonments were wrong, and the power some people had over the lives and deaths of others was also wrong."

I listened to her soft voice with the utmost attention because I'd never before heard anything like it. At that moment Madame Wogdeman was far more intriguing than the Russian princesses of theatrical productions and French romances, divested of their ancestral jewels, dancing in Parisian cabarets or serving in coffeehouses, adjusting themselves to a new way of life with the proficiency of well-trained muscles and elegance of fine breeding.

"Yes," she repeated with some effort, as though straining to remember something. "You shouldn't believe everything they say about us in the European newspapers."

"In that case, why don't you want to go back?"

"Of course, it sounds odd. For in those terrible times I lost none of my closest relatives, no one was killed before my eyes, I wasn't imprisoned or interrogated by the Cheka,[76] nothing was even taken from me, I was never hungry—not once, when others were dying of starvation… I don't know if you understand me: *I always had something to eat…*"

I found it hard to say I understood.[77] But she suddenly realized she'd said too much, should not have said what she'd just said. She regained control of her feelings and her manner cooled.

"The sacrifices were dreadful, sacrifices it's not even possible to contemplate. So I was waiting… But later I couldn't wait any longer…"

The same thing in her struck me as before, as when she spoke so strangely, almost ceremonially, about Fuchs that time we were in Miss Norah's room. Yes, that was what was the keenest in her: her understanding of what it meant to be morally defeated. Something already attuned within responded to Fuchs, like a string reverberating inside a musical instrument in response to a sounding note.

"I am not saying nothing has changed," repeated Madame Wogdeman. "No, I am not saying that. A great deal has changed. But these things, however, have remained the same: war, imprisonments, and the power of some over the lives and deaths of others…"

I heard her out but said nothing. What could I say? How could I console her when she herself thought and felt like that? When she had suffered more from injuries inflicted than others suffer from injuries sustained? When she had once believed in the righteousness of the cause, and could not now bear the reality of the victorious revolution… And had come as far away as our villa in her moral bankruptcy, so as at least not to see or so as to forget…

Meanwhile, at Madame de Carfort's request, little Sossé read out her translation, which I already knew, of the Armenian prayer:

Lord, have mercy upon us
Lord, have mercy upon us.
Holy Trinity, send us peace on earth,
Grant health to the sick!
Console the suffering!

"Only up to there," said Sossé, staring with her solemn childlike eyes into the face of Monsieur de Flèche. "Because we are not free to pray for anything…"

"Yes, only up to there," he replied. And smiled at her in sorrow and gratitude.

Madame Wogdeman sat with her thin hands clasped around her elbows, while her eyes were fixed on a point beyond the open window of Sossé's room, as far away as possible: on the summits of the Dents du Midi beneath the starry, spring night sky.

"*Il n'y a de vraie révolution que morale,*" she whispered, echoing the words of Duhamel.[78]

"For otherwise, wouldn't revolution just be calling the same things by a different name?"

32

It so happened that both Est and the Saint-Alberts left our company at more or less the same time.

As far as Est was concerned, we thought initially he'd simply died. Such things usually take place very quietly in such places. And since Madame de Carfort did not appear at table for several days—which happened regularly anyway because of her neuralgia—we didn't discuss Est with anyone.

Instead everyone was intrigued by the Saint-Alberts.

One day they just disappeared. The sun-drenched, flowery room where they used to sit stood empty for two days. Then a young couple, recently arrived, whom no one knew and who Carrizales likewise said were definitely not married, took their place.

When questioned, Charles said that Monsieur and Madame Saint-Albert had departed suddenly as a result of a letter they'd received from Paris. But no one trusted this as being reliable, for Charles spoke with an air, typical of sanatoria, whereby saying someone had "departed" implied they had "died." On the other hand, Mademoiselle Hovsepian maintained Madame Saint-Albert suffered from heart problems and the mountain air had done her no good, so her husband had taken the sick woman somewhere in the valley.

Once the conversation turned to this, Mademoiselle Alice smiled to me across the table with a knowing expression. But I didn't grasp immediately what she meant.

There was some truth however in the letter from Paris. That evening in little Sossé's room, Monsieur de Flèche told us he'd read in the newspapers of the death of Madame Saint-Albert's first husband, who was also—as everyone knew—the uncle of her second husband. Their sudden departure might have been prompted by family considerations.

"It's hard to imagine they were invited to the funeral," said Carrizales, pretending to be shocked.

Of course, if we'd really wanted to find out, we could surely have done so. But our curiosity did not stretch that far. It didn't occur to any of us to properly question Monsieur de Flèche, who had known them previously and might know something now, or Mademoiselle Hovsepian, with whom they had perhaps been on the most intimate terms. Everyone referred to the whole affair with a hint of jocular light-heartedness, mingled with slight distaste at the undoubted scandal provoked by the very presence of such an ill-matched pair.

Only Mademoiselle Hovsepian was unable to hide her surprise, as well as resentment, that the Saint-Alberts, who had not said good-bye to anyone, had not left a few words of explanation even for her.

"I know she wanted to leave a long time ago," said the Armenian. "She didn't feel right here…"

Mademoiselle Alice went out for the whole of the next day on an excursion with Curchaud. She reappeared only the following morning after breakfast and at once announced she had something to tell me.

"I had an immensely interesting conversation with Monsieur de Flèche—he made such a strong impression on me and I think he's struck by me too."

We were sitting in the flower-bedecked room, where the Saint-Alberts had once sat, and Alice spoke to me with her usual gaiety and lack of sophistication:

"There's something about me which seems to have an extraordinary effect on men. Because I thought Monsieur de Flèche was cold and inaccessible, preoccupied perhaps with the Armenian. Meanwhile he too… He told me that he pitied what might happen to my poor young soul in this cattle-market of a world, that I'm going to the bad, that my strange nature draws me too powerfully toward the joys of life. He was uncommonly frank. He said there were many things in me he didn't like, and yet…"

She laughed out loud.

"He was concerned about the Saint-Alberts. Evidently he must have been thinking it through."

"Thinking what through?"

"Don't you see? Her sudden illness was just a sham, a comedy! She did it deliberately, removed him from here deliberately so it would be impossible for us to see each other. First of all she refused to leave his side. They were seen constantly and everywhere together, which made it impossible to exchange a couple of words with him. Ah! It was such a simple game, I saw through it immediately. And then later, when I finally sent him a note saying I absolutely had to see him, and begged him to name the time and place himself, he replied in the silliest fashion that we could meet in the evening after dinner in the lounge, here—that is, in the presence of a whole bunch of people! In front of Curchaud, who would then make scenes, and in front of her too! He couldn't have written it himself, you understand—she must have made him write it. And so I made fun of him when he asked me in the evening what I wished to say to him. He pretended to sulk, and kept looking at her anxiously to see if she was watching us. I had a great laugh at his expense, but Monsieur de Flèche told me I'm wicked..."

Mademoiselle Alice's candor, and also the memory of our joint expedition, meant I indeed began to associate the departure of Monsieur and Madame Saint-Albert in my imagination with the dangerous disposition of the captivating Russian. But I must confess that on this occasion my powers of penetration led me up the garden path. All too often things are quite different in reality from how they appear on the surface.

That same day in the evening, for the first time in several days, Madame de Carfort came down to dinner. Her beauty, rendered more delicate by ill health, seemed to me once again marvelously composed and noble.

"Est is no longer with us," she spoke first. Her eyelids, narrowly encircling her wonderful dark eyes, were thinner than usual and imparted an expression of weariness to her gaze.

"He died?" I asked.

"No! He was still alive when he left. His father came to collect him. But it's impossible he'll survive the journey. They shouldn't have allowed it," she added sternly. "But *they* usually happily consent to the departure of the sick, when *it* is already certain..."

She sighed.

"The last time I saw him, I went alone, summoned especially by him through Sister. It was the only time he didn't joke at all. He told me in all seriousness he couldn't die here, that he did not want to, that it was a total impossibility."

She lowered her lids so it wasn't so obvious her eyes were clouded by tears. And in an odd, hard, dry voice entirely foreign to her, she said:

"I suggested it to him myself, and on reflection he agreed. A priest was called and Est was baptized before his death..."

Looking at Madame de Carfort, I could be absolutely sure she was capable of doing such a thing and would not have hesitated for a second.

"Immediately afterwards he was driven to the station. Just consider: how strange it is, how incalculably significant, that he could die *only in Romania*..."

33

I had observed that with each of our acquaintances we walked somewhere different and talked about different subjects.

With Mr and Mrs Vigil we always went in one direction, making our way to the right—into the forest where a picturesque little footpath had been gouged out of the rock, fenced off above the gorge by an ordinary, attractive little hedge of young spruce trunks. We carried our Kodak cameras, took photographs, and later compared them among ourselves to see whose had come out best. The forest was magical beneath the snows; every snapshot seemed an illustration to a fairy tale. And later on when the snows melted, on a sunny day, you might think it was already high summer inside the forest—because there was nothing there except the spruce trees, and on the ground only dry needle litter and pink-grey rocks, which never changed at all.

The forest and the path hewn into it, bordered by the little hedge, ended after a while and opened onto an exposed sloping pasture, bordered by a normal fence, not unlike the ones at home. On the edge of the pasture, right above the sheer cliff, there stood a small wooden chalet, very old, with a strange decorative balcony, an ancient well, boarded over by planks, and a single huge tree, still denuded of leaves, which leaned at an angle over the precipice.

The chalet was not entirely shut up. Through the tiny window, pieces of basic furniture and milking utensils could be seen. But no one lived there anymore. Later in the year the cows would wander up from below with their herdsman.

You could sit comfortably on the planks covering the low well, and stare before you in amazement. Because this old, faded, empty little house stood as though suspended over chasms of airy nothingness, above an arena of the most magnificent views—also like a cottage in a fairy tale.

Ten paces from our feet the sloping pasture ended abruptly; and it was as though the whole of palpable reality also ended. For just beyond that edge began the milky, radiant azure of far distances, the vast enormity of space, the fathomless depths of the world fashioned into mountains and valleys, waters and fields, forests and towns. How could you believe in it, straight away, at once, when all you had immediately before you was a scrap of stunted yellow grass or that insignificant little bush by the fence to the right, thrusting out its meager side-branch higher into the blue sky than those farthest mountain peaks…?

It was a place to which you had to constantly return, and about which you thought when far-removed from it. And we always returned precisely to that same spot with Mr and Mrs Vigil.

Mr Vigil, as I already explained, was a keen huntsman and had plenty to say on the topic. He was interested in anything remotely connected with it. He loved the natural world and its beauty but precisely from this angle, on this level—as the habitat of various animals which allowed themselves to be tracked down, shadowed, and killed. His year was divided not into spring and summer, autumn and winter, but into the various shooting seasons.

And so with the Vigils we usually discussed hunting, compared the shooting traditions in their country and ours, discussed different types of game-bird and other animals for killing. Dogs were likewise an enormous topic of conversation, which was simply never exhausted. We also talked a lot about photography, different cameras and types of photographic plate, and photographs that had been unsuccessful. Mr and Mrs Vigil were young people, cheerful, full of life and so made good company on such a walk.

On the other hand, it was not possible to enjoy pleasant conversations with them on other subjects. If we tried to talk about books, for instance, then Mr Vigil never read a single thing, and Mrs Vigil liked best the novels of Baroness Orczy. If we talked about people, then the Vigils possessed a vast number of prejudices of various kinds. They despised almost every other nation, made fun of the French and the Spanish, loathed Negroes, and considered Irishmen to be brigands and murderers.

And they weren't the only ones! I had always imagined Miss Norah to be quite different from the Vigils—sensitive to everything, kindly disposed toward everyone, not only empathizing acutely with the fate of Mademoiselle Sossé but even able to fret over the fate of a man like Fuchs!

Yet she too surprised me.

I once borrowed from her an unusual English novel, in which the attitude of the Irish to England was presented not only in objective terms but with unmistakable sympathy.[79]

"Did you like the book?" I asked.

"Oh, very much!" she cried with her usual enthusiasm.

But then she reflected for a moment and added:

"I feel very sorry for the Irish, truly very sorry. But they are an unruly lot."

"It's hard not to be unruly in the circumstances," I said.

"Yes, naturally. But it's odd, you know, it's somehow stronger than me: I hate them."

"What?" I was astonished. I thought I'd misunderstood her.

"*I hate them,*" she repeated quite distinctly, staring me straight in the eye with a look both frank and serene.

34

Like the sea, distant mountains have that marvelous unreality of lighting and color, impermanence of perspective, elusiveness of contours and boundaries, in which nothing is prejudged—and can always still become all over again, anew. Nothing is irrevocably known for sure, and everything is once more possible.

From out of the mingling of white, pink, and golden haze, from the pale green windows opening into the sky between cracks in the clouds, from the shimmering brass petals showering the evening summits and valleys, from the lilac downiness of the light, from all intensities of blue through the palest to the deepest azure to the totally black—there emerges what is perhaps not entirely real, but nevertheless potentially real: life's goodness.

One day we went down to the valley by car.

The great twists in the white road straightened out once we were driving across the flat, green-carpeted fluvial plain. On either side rose walls of rock, expansive and protective, while distant chains of snow-capped peaks peeped out above the clouds.

We sped steadily along in the silence and peace—our onward rush stirring up a sleepy warm wind, which whirled and fluttered in our faces yet did not disturb a leaf hanging in the sun on a wayside branch. The white dust leapt to right and left from under the wheels, pursued us for a moment and then fell back to earth behind us, unable to fly farther.

Until on the left-hand side, beyond the trees, there shone the smooth blue light of Lake Geneva's peaceful water.

We drove past the gardens of Villeneuve and a small, ornate castle rising above the glassy water among clumps of green—the unlikely setting for Byron's gloomy legend.[80] Then through the streets of lakeside towns bathed in sunlight, below the flowered walls of villas and palaces, until we arrived at our familiar jetty in the corner of the lake.

Several hours went by and evening came. We rowed over the darkening water. The mountains by the shore became shrouded in greyish or navy-tinted shades of azure, and ceased to be real. A single yellow shaft of light from the jetty streamed constantly toward us, trickling across the surface of the lake—yet expiring before it reached us in a few floating, fading, watery bursts.

I rowed with my face to the west—facing that side of the world where heaven and earth opened before me their rose and purple depths.

Identical dark cloudlets hung in the translucent pink gold of air and water—their reflection in the lake's surface seeming like clusters of damp violets. The glassy radiance, rocking gently to and fro, reached to the very side of our black boat, slipping down and away with each smack of the oars.

"But on that side, look, it's already night!"[81]

Yes, I knew, but there it was dreadful, awesome. I didn't want to look, didn't even want to turn my head. A milky, deep-blue darkness was engulfing the world, pouring over it with a soft rustling and then hardening, while the liquid pewter sheet of the lake grew flat and flimsy, weighed down by the burden of darkness.

"Do you remember how at night, on the lake at Rajgród,[82] you were afraid to row to the woods on the far bank?"

"Yes, I remember."

"And we had to turn back from the middle of the lake…"

I still endeavored to watch the sunset, where the last tiny bars of lilac and gold were fading from water and sky.

Many lamplights were now streaming toward us from the shore in narrow, trembling, watery beams. While the surface they rode over was pitch black.

"Yes. And I remember Lake Gopło and Lakes Kań and Białe,[83] where we also rowed at night. Here it's so beautiful, but there it was miraculous."

There and here: we two. Thus we stored up the beauty of the world in our hearts and in our memory.

Because in relation to every beautiful thing in the world, here and there—and more precisely *there,* where we once were and where we would return—that unchanging fact of existence would continue to repeat itself and persist: we two.[84]

The boat moved slowly forward, as the shafts of light on the water from streetlamps on the shore retreated before us, growing shorter and shorter, plummeting to the depths of the lake.

We maneuvered at an angle into a narrow, black space in a long line of boats. We struck the boards of the jetty. The shadowy figure of a man seized the side of the boat with his hand.

Among the dark greenery of the gardens a stone statue shone dimly. A large tram rumbled by beneath a wall. Beyond the trees the streets of the town blazed with light.

35

Before we reached the place where our chauffeur was to wait, we met Monsieur Saint-Albert. He was coming down the hill toward us along the quiet floodlit street. In his hand he carried light parcels of sweets or fruit.

His greeting was warm and unconstrained. He did not seem in the least embarrassed by the unexpected encounter—despite the manner of our parting not being entirely clear. He simply made no mention of it, no justifications.

"My wife is here too, she's with me here," he said, as though we might have supposed otherwise. "Her health is still not quite right. She's suffering from a weakening of the heart muscle, so they're recommending as little movement as possible. She has to rest up."

We told him to pass on our greetings but did not propose a visit. Neither did he suggest it, and happily accepted the news that we'd be leaving in half an hour.

I noticed that he scarcely smiled, that it was still harder for him to smile to the end than it had been before.

So they had gone no further than this! Just to be no longer in our villa, just to get away from the people up there!

Still influenced by what had been said concerning their departure, I somehow couldn't believe Madame Saint-Albert was unwell. After all, she'd looked splendid the whole time, and never given the impression of being tired on our walks.

Despite my desire to disbelieve it, Mademoiselle Alice's explanation seemed the most likely—perhaps because it was expressed with such self-belief, allowing no room for doubt.

Not knowing what was really going on with the Saint-Alberts, we said nothing about our meeting when we got home.

Meanwhile, soon after our return, I received a letter from Madame Saint-Albert.

She wrote that she was still unwell and totally alone, and implored me fervently to visit her, should we plan another trip to the lake. Obviously, I agreed without hesitation.

When I saw Madame Saint-Albert, I had to believe in her illness. The blinds were drawn in her hotel room, and the interior had a warm pinkish glow from the sunlight shining in from outside. Madame Saint-Albert lay on her bed fully clothed and did not rise when I entered. It shocked me to see her lying with her legs crossed on the satin counterpane. I thought at first she wore pale-colored stockings, but then realized she had court shoes directly on her bare feet.

Indeed, the style of her illness was as though not properly organized, insufficiently established. I could be in no doubt, however. Her face had shrunk and her eyes were encircled by dark shadows. The expression of her mouth had also changed, and in a quite specific way. Namely, her lips were shriveled, grown thin and flabby.

"I can no longer lie still," she told me. "But as soon as I get up, I immediately feel worse."

Thus we talked for a while about doctors and cures. Until Madame Saint-Albert simply said:

"To me it's all the same what they're saying about us. I have no idea if they've found out or not. It's Saint-Albert who attaches so much importance to it, he's still such a child…"

"Everyone knows you were recommended a spell down below. It's a common thing not to be able to tolerate the high altitude."

She scrutinized me closely, and added:

"Well, yes. But beforehand I was well."

I said nothing. For God's sake, it was not up to me to explain the reason for their departure.

"Yes," she said again. "Saint-Albert attaches great importance to it. So I agreed. Though it's all the same to me where I live, or indeed where I die."

She broke off to take a deep breath.

"Seeing as it can't be there… Seeing as it can no longer be there…"

Since it seemed she was having difficulty drawing breath again, I didn't want to exhaust her with conversation. But she refused to let me go.

"I ought to explain certain things to you, my totally childish marriage. I'd prefer it if you weren't surprised… For my behavior can be explained purely by the coming together of certain circumstances, by the situation…"

So I listened, since that was what she wanted, since she had to talk about it to someone at any cost…

"To me, my marriage seems like an affront to morality. How can I put it: like something contrary to nature? For more than ten years I never noticed his existence beside me, that little Saint-Albert, his childish adoration. He used to come to us every vacation. He was like our own son, would spend weeks or months with us—and then leave again. I was his aunt or almost his mother—a bad mother, who didn't know how to love him. I was the one who first told him he could stay in the lounge when guests came to visit. I can't think of him without irritation, without disgust. It's so shameful and embarrassing…"

Madame Saint-Albert no longer lay on her back but curled up on her side, her feet tucked under the hem of her dressing gown. The cast-off shoes remained on the counterpane. She felt cold, so I handed her a large woolen shawl that lay on the couch. She didn't want to undress, however, and get under the counterpane. She wanted to talk.

"Things changed only during some dreadful outings on horseback. By that time, I always rode alone, that is—alone or with Saint-Albert.

"Our locality differs in color from any other region in France. The air is strangely whitish and obscures the whole world. The green of the vineyards, the flowers in spring—everything is as though filtered through a veil of white tulle. And it seems as if the weather is never entirely fine—even though the sun shines and there are no clouds in the sky. I don't know if it's a kind of delicate haze or some sort of dust that refracts every ray of light. For fifteen years we went everywhere together—on horseback or by car, along roads that always ended in a grove of flowering bushes by a riverbank. And we always admired the whiteness of the air—the air, which everywhere else is invisible. For fifteen long years we were always a little surprised by it, however. But afterwards, I rode only by myself or with Saint-Albert. And just as I was capable—as I choked back my tears—of embracing the neck of my horse or the trunk of some young tree, so I was capable of embracing one day the neck of Saint-Albert.

"...So that's how it happened, but it doesn't exonerate me, or put things right. It's immoral how I prey on his youth with what remains of my life. Everywhere he goes he drags me along, pulls me back to the surface. Thanks to him I'm able to travel, walk over mountains, come and go—live. But I no longer want this. I want peace, and death. Isn't it understandable at last? Isn't it obvious?

"His love torments me; his love is an *affront* to me. If it were not for him, I would no longer be alive. It was he who saved me—for the second time..."

36

Twilight was descending on little Sossé's room, full of playthings, books, and flowers. I had not noticed she'd made any movement—when suddenly, at a given moment, a single lamp wrapped in pink silk began to glow on the wall above a large lilac. And the tiny white starlets of the lilac sprays turned pale pink.

In her thin fragile fingers Sossé clutched an ivory crucifix which she had recently received as a gift from Monsieur de Flèche.

She confessed to me in her soft sing-song voice that she was happy now, truly happy.

"Why now?"

She was happy now, but before: how she had suffered... For only recently had she regained that greatest good—the grace of faith.

"Yes, because I tried to live without God—and was punished for it. How could I ever imagine it was possible? I lived through years of such terrible yearning for Him, long years of uncertainty and doubt. How much I suffered then...."

I was hearing Sossé's complaint for the first time. But she spoke of her past sorrow only to give me an idea of her present happiness.

"And I was seeking God all the time. I sought Him in vain among my tortured thoughts—until the day I found Him."

She stopped talking, lost in thought.

"No, it wasn't like that. It wasn't I who found God. It was He who took pity on my childish tears, on my weakness and destitution—and sought me out in my darkness, where I was stretching out my arms to Him in vain..."

She smiled in shy rapture as she spoke.

"It began a long time ago," she said after a pause, "began already then... From the terrible questions that arise when you see such suffering and fear. When you witness evil... Because if I'd really been able then to believe that what happened to Armenia was some sort of exception, some sort of incomprehensible mistake... If I'd been sure that it contradicted the order of the world, threatened the harmony of the world... But it was in keeping with the nature of things, it was like everything else, like wars, like what was going on in the various colonies, what was happening in Ireland... It was even worse, but it was not intrinsically different. Do you understand? *It was not different.* And it was this that I couldn't bear, this that shook me—and distanced me from God..."

Terror now shone in her eyes, always so full of such timid, astonished sweetness.

"I have been thinking a lot about animals, which are silent, not surprised by anything. They have no moral imperatives. Their hatred and struggles, cruelty and suffering do not stem from their sins. Neither do their strange crimes and victims...[85] The whole of fragrant, singing nature is pervaded by torment and pain..."

She didn't want to be interrupted. She wanted to talk.

"How good it is to die peacefully and gradually in bed, when we think of that, when we compare. What peace there is, security even in such a death, *n'est-ce pas?*

"For the sufferings humans inflict on animals are less cruel than the sufferings animals inflict on themselves.[86] Less cruel, and there are less of them. What terrible sorrow there is in the fact that animals have to prey on the lives of other animals, that they can't—aren't able to do otherwise. What sorrow in the fear that permeates nature, in the fearfulness of birds… Fear, after all, is the only self-defense many possess, fear and suffering— nothing more. How many animals don't defend themselves at all, having no illusions, no hope?! They just run away, or don't know even how to run away. And until the last moment—apart from suffering—they also know terror, only to perish in the vulture's claws or jackal's teeth.

"Animals are capable of experiencing not only panic and suffering, but also love. I remember a strange thing, in reality quite trivial. About rats. They were living in the hen house—at home, when we were still there—and taking eggs from the roosts. A trap was laid and eventually one rat was caught. But the next day another egg vanished. And a few days later the maid found, in the middle of the roost, seven tiny dead rats dragged there on purpose and abandoned. Do you know what had happened? The rat caught in the trap was a female, who had been suckling those little ones. And after her death, the male was left knowing his little ones would gradually die of starvation without their mother. And when they had all died, he removed them from the den with his teeth in order to show—I don't know—his pain and the wrong done to him, to frighten people with the sight, so terrible to him… Or perhaps he had gone crazy and so he removed those dead children…"

No, I didn't want to hear this.

"Why do you remember such things?" I said. "You shouldn't think about it."

She glanced at me sadly, almost as if asking for a favor. And after a while she said in an odd voice:

"But I don't talk about everything—everything I remember."

120

She broke off and lowered her eyes—almost ashamed, as though by these very words she had already said too much.

Throughout all this time, as she spoke,[87] she clutched and rotated the crucifix in her intertwined hands—in the same way she used to clutch and rotate her playthings. And there was a strange solemnity in this childish juxtaposition.

"God does not wish for evil, although he allows it to exist. That's what Madame de Carfort says. To her, the idea that God might desire evil is a great sin. She is strong and never doubts. And she is good. She was saying that the world is a harmony, a strange and wonderful balance between good and evil. She knows how to find good in suffering; for her, the perpetual transformation of the world is both beautiful and comforting.—Oh, I was thinking about this all night, trying to find solace in her words, consolation for my agony. But I couldn't. There is no consolation in the world. The world is deadly serious and afflicted by suffering. And in this suffering, which does not ennoble, there is no fulfillment, no harmony…

"Then I was talking about the same thing with Monsieur Totsky. He admires the world in all its detail and entirety, with both its good and evil, beauty and ugliness. He accepts the world—but in a way I cannot trust, in a way that doesn't convince me. And yet I cannot understand this. Monsieur Totsky is at peace—he doesn't need harmony in order to praise, admire or even love reality… According to him, the whole transcendental world, the world beyond—the object and aim of our faith—is contained within the bounds of reality. Can you understand that?"

She looked at me questioningly…

"Do you understand? For him, faith is what reality has already discovered for itself within itself—and then elevated above and beyond itself. It is the majestic luxury of nature—something with which nature exceeds itself, its flourishing and crowning glory—and its only justification. When a wolf howls though it is

no longer hungry, or a bird sings when it's already built its nest—
it's there that reality's longing for something beyond itself begins.
It is human sadness amid the greatest happiness, what endows
human suffering with beauty, the necessity in humans to wor-
ship Goodness and Love beyond themselves. And all the things
in which human beings have clothed their death, honored, and
made it splendid.—I told Totsky: according to you, God is on
this side. You do not believe in a God outside of man… And only
then did Monsieur de Flèche arrive…"

Sossé fell silent. Or maybe she wasn't ready yet to talk about
him. She returned to Monsieur Totsky.

"He often seems spiteful, or insensitive. Indeed. Often he's
even tactless. But he is very good. And his goodness substitutes
for faith… He believes in the progress of the world, he believes in
the good.[88] But I am too weak for this kind of faith. I cannot be
alone faced by what is to come—and by what already is."

Now Sossé began to talk about Monsieur de Flèche.

"He was brought here the first time by Mademoiselle Hovsepian. He likes the same books as I do, likes music. And he too
is unwell.

"We knew so little about each other. And when I told him that
thinking about the sufferings of the world had robbed me of my
faith, he was astonished. He asked: 'And so you don't remember
Christ on the Mount of Olives, the God who suffered?'

"I remembered, but then I couldn't understand it: understand
that if God, who is the highest form of Love, is supposed to be
Almighty, then…

"Monsieur de Flèche asked me again: 'Don't you think He suf-
fers when He's unable to conquer the evil of the world and the
sufferings of people? He is the highest form of Love, which has
yet to accomplish its ultimate goals. And relying on the human
race, He seeks in people and loves in them precisely their agony,
suffered as the result of evil. Because only through people can
the world He created accomplish good.'

"Then Monsieur de Flèche told me that perfect Love is not almighty. And that the way to comprehending this truth is via the Mount of Olives, via the words of Christ's prayer..."

She confided this to me in a whisper as if it were a closely guarded secret, clasping her thin little hands together as though in prayer.

"Not only did the man in Him suffer, outstretched on the cross, pierced by the sword; God also suffered in Him—because of His powerlessness to overcome evil. Besides He took martyrdom upon Himself, and consented not only to His own agony but also to the evil of those who were to inflict it upon Him. Would it have happened thus, if He'd been able to do otherwise?"

37

"Do you know the Saint-Alberts are here, in M...?"[89]

"Yes, I do know," I said.

Mademoiselle Alice was not looking her usual self. We were sitting next to one another on a bench beneath a villa wall, watching from above as the cog train made its way down into the valley and over the viaduct.

"I've endured such painful things, I've no idea myself *how* I got through it. Monsieur de Flèche can demand anything of me. It was he who told me that Madame Saint-Albert poisoned herself here, that they managed to save her, that she poisoned herself because of me. Yes, I used to see Saint-Albert now and then because I found him so enormously attractive. His smile has something about it that makes it irresistible. His smile but also his gaze. When they look at you, his eyes seem to stroke, caress, kiss you even. Am I to be blamed for liking him so much? Anyway, it's all entirely unimportant to me now, but before it was something wonderful. However, on the request of Monsieur de Flèche, I immediately wrote that letter and handed it to Saint-Albert myself at our last meeting. What more could I do? Maybe she found my letter. Maybe he told her himself—I have no idea. Maybe that was the reason… But I already wanted to break with him then, she should have understood that."

Mademoiselle Alice spoke rapidly, as she usually did, in a manner quite self-sufficient. She expected neither wonderment nor approbation. It was enough for her that I listened.

"But now it's something different. I am totally different," she said, still not looking at me, although the last carriage of the little train had already disappeared over a ridge in the valley.

"I didn't know I existed at all till now, although I knew him, though I'd seen him a long time ago. I didn't suspect at all. I'm not even sure he likes me, yet I think of him all the time. Day and night are full of the thought of him. I love him, I simply love him; nothing can save me from it. I think about him not with my thoughts, but with the joy of my whole body. When I'm totally alone, I'm always smiling. I yearn for him constantly, even when he's standing right beside me. And when he is right beside me, I'm no longer free, unable to smile, can't say anything to him honestly. I don't even know if he knows. He's so noble-minded, so indifferent. He loves that Armenian, that's for sure. He converted her, I already know everything. He believes in God and in goodness."

Yes, things were bad with her. Her genuine, unmistakable suffering—the suffering born of passion—was clearly visible in the anxiety of her eyes, in the doleful expression of her mouth, in the unconscious wringing of her hands whenever she spoke.

"What a terrible delight to look into his eyes! His eyes, so cold and unresponsive."

She was talking now as if I no longer sat beside her. And she was not in the least embarrassed by anything she said.

"I am hungry in my love. I'm in agony and understand nothing. I want his kiss and yet I'm afraid to touch his hand. I don't know what to say to him, I hide yet give myself away. I run away from him though he never pursues me, but I catch myself doing it and come running back. I'm constantly composing in advance the words I'll say to him—and then forget them the moment I see him. Whenever I'm with him I deliberately act in a way guaranteed to offend him, pretend I'm still interested in Carrizales or someone else. I flirt. Curchaud has never been so sure I'll go with him to Phnom Penh. And yet any conversation, any smile, any time spent with any other man is such a strain and such torture. Because anything beyond him is dreadful and intolerable, the whole world beyond him is simply unbearable."

She covered her eyes with her hand for a moment as if shielding them from the sun, which at that moment flooded the whole marvelous world before us with its light.

"When I can't actually see someone, I can always imagine them. It's enough to cover my eyes and knit my brow—and I will always see them even if it's just for a second. I can always imagine anyone, except Monsieur de Flèche…"

Helpless, she dropped her hand.

"I *know* what he's like, but I *don't see* him. I know the shape of his forehead and eyebrows; I know how he looks at things, slightly moving his pale lashes. I remember he has a gentle voice. But I yearn in vain for his image. And when he stands right beside me, I also yearn for him—as I told you…"

She lapsed into silence, staring now at something straight ahead of her.

"I used to be so much surer of myself. It never entered my head to be embarrassed by my appearance. Now I feel hideous before him, I'm ashamed of my face. I can't walk when he's walking behind me in case he thinks I'm ungainly…"

Well, no. Monsieur de Flèche would certainly not have thought that. On that score I could have put her mind completely at rest. But again I did not respond, sensing Mademoiselle Alice did not expect it.

"There is so much in me, so much to give him. My arms stretch out toward him of their own accord. I am waiting only for a gesture on his part, to run to him like a summoned animal.

"But it's entirely unnecessary to him. He has no idea at all, doesn't even imagine…"

Her voice wavered but did not break. She was not someone who cried easily. But nor was she someone who easily suffered. She was deeply surprised by her suffering, knew neither its methods nor the means to cope with it.

She was bewildered by it, in love for the first time…

"In the beginning I thought nothing of it, I was simply glad he existed, that I could see him, listen to what he was saying. In the beginning there was real joy in it—there was happiness. But now… Even his kindness is terrible to me, because if he were to guess how much I suffer, then he would surely sympathize with me, he would feel sorry for me… Everything in him is a humiliation to me. Not only that sick Sossé, but every other woman he speaks to, is a torture to me—and I never thought myself a jealous type. Yesterday I saw him from a distance walking with Madame de Carfort.—And it occurred to me for the first time that she was pretty, certainly prettier than me… What am I to do? How can I save myself? Is it better if he guesses about me, or if he never finds out?"

Suddenly, Mademoiselle Alice turned to me and looked me straight in the eye. I had the impression she'd only just noticed me, because at that moment I was necessary to her. My *experience* of life was necessary to her.

"What do you think?" she asked. "Is it possible that such a thing, that all this can really be only *one-sided*? That there is no place at all in his life for everything I feel for him, could bring to him with myself? That this terrible potential happiness is no happiness to him? That I am dying of rapture and agony as I look into his eyes, and that he feels nothing? Is such a thing really possible?"

This time she demanded an answer from me, demanded it as if I were passing sentence.

I knew only too well that what to her was inconceivable was entirely possible. But when I looked at her lovely young face, black eyes tormented by love, parched lips breathing desire; when I saw her hands wrung in despair, straining toward a caress—I had neither the certainty nor the coldness to respond.

I remained silent, full of unease. Because this time I was thinking of fragile, sick little Sossé, kept alive perhaps only by the affection of Monsieur de Flèche.

"I don't know," I said after a long pause. "One can never tell."

We rose from our bench in order to return home. Mademoiselle Alice walked beside me—tall, conspicuous, drawing toward her the eyes of all men, but now totally unaware of it. She stared ahead of her at little stones on the road, yet her lips were smiling involuntarily—because she was thinking about him.

38

Early one morning I heard the following words, permeated with sentimental longing and, one might say, melancholy:

"It's already getting warmer, the worms are emerging from the soil, there's plenty to eat…"

"My God, what are you saying?" I asked in alarm.

No, no, it was nothing, luckily not a symptom that might prompt justified fears. It simply meant fewer and fewer choucas were showing up at our morning banquets and the bread soaked in milk often lay for hours on the balustrade before being finally eaten. And this was because the earth, denuded of snow, in bloom and turning green, now provided sufficient nourishment for all the birds.

This reminded us that the term prescribed for our stay in that beautiful place had elapsed and it was time to return to our far-away home.

The mountains gradually emptied as the season drew to a close. From our villa, Mr and Mrs Vigil had already departed, while Monsieur Verdy, whom the mountains had not restored to health this time as they had in his youth, was also preparing to go home.

He sorely missed his grandsons. But he had lost all hope of living to see the older boy succeed him in the factory, as he had once been succeeded by his only son who never returned from the Marne. Since the time he lost his son, he'd no longer felt equal to carrying on the work himself. He departed sad and disappointed, just as old and helpless as when he came.

Lady Malden had left some time before. The Italian, Signore Costa, to whom Miss Norah could no longer cry *buon giorno,* had also gone.

Monsieur Totsky was constantly on the point of leaving but put off his departure from day to day. In the evenings we always listened for a while to his beautiful playing.

Naturally, it was hard for him to leave the place where Madame de Carfort was to remain for the entire summer. Only in the winter would she be allowed to return to her broiling Morocco, which was so detrimental to her health.

One day he finally left. We watched to the very last moment as he stood at the carriage window of the cog train descending into the abyss, waving his handkerchief for as long as we could still see him.

The Armenians, on the other hand, who had nowhere to go, did not leave. Nor did Madame Wogdeman, to whom it was all the same wherever she was. Nor did the unpopular Herr Fuchs, whose health had not improved at all.

Monsieur Curchaud had also not departed, as though he were still waiting for Mademoiselle Alice, who followed Monsieur de Flèche everywhere with her burning eyes yet laughed provocatively toward Curchaud with lips throbbing in agony.

And Monsieur de Flèche too had not yet departed.

"It's sad even, you know," little Sossé said to me once. "I have so much to be grateful for to Monsieur de Flèche and feel so much friendship for him, it troubles me. He stays up here, but he could leave if he wanted to. His cure is over, he is healthy. But still he doesn't leave. He keeps putting off his departure."

She hesitated—unsure, fearful—she, who was truly incapable of saying everything to the end.

"For a long time I couldn't drum up the courage, didn't dare mention it. Only yesterday… Yesterday I begged him not to wait any longer—I'm no longer able to recover…"

39

The thing Mademoiselle Alice found so hard to believe indeed proved to be impossible. Her enamored eyes blazed all too powerfully with the strength of her feelings, her mouth cried out to be kissed all too eloquently.

"It's happiness impossible to bear," she told me laughing. "The whole world is filled with this one thing—and I am simply suffocating, I can't catch my breath…"

That's how it was with her. She walked among us like a living torch. Her smile, her words, her game—were a constant, never-ending triumph.

Whenever she saw Monsieur de Flèche she would walk directly up to him without taking her eyes off him—following the single straight line of her own gaze. Any obstacles between them—objects or people—had to step aside of their own accord to let her pass. I don't know if this were really the case—but it was hard not to imagine it otherwise. And every one of us sensed it, we all moved to one side, walked away, vanished—whenever they met. We all experienced the awful desolation of someone else's happiness.

Meanwhile nothing had changed with little Sossé, at least on the surface. None of her friends failed to turn up to her room during the habitual short visiting hours.

And Monsieur de Flèche too was always there—smiling tenderly at her words and glances, surrendering totally to the effect of her unique, childish, fatal spell.

I remembered, moreover, how a sudden pallor overspread his normally placid face whenever he caught sight of Mademoiselle Alice in a crowd of people.

Now I often watched him carefully—and have to admit his whole attitude toward little Sossé inspired confidence and sympathy. He was not someone capable of unintentionally causing suffering, someone unaware of the harm he could inflict. His kindness was wise and considerate.

And yet I found it hard to dismiss my fear over Sossé's fate, if she were to find out about the other thing, if the other thing were to become evident and somehow official.

Monsieur de Flèche was so serene and self-possessed it was impossible to detect whether some great internal struggle were taking place within him, or not; whether or not two quite different, equally seductive worlds were vying for control. Sometimes I thought perhaps the two feelings did not cross paths, truly existing alongside one another and somehow managing to persist in harmony within the one man. But for how long could it go on?

Among the short verses that Sossé once showed me, shyly and modestly, there was one that now sprang to mind. It went as follows:

> *Vous regrettez que j'aie tant de frêles papillons dans mes yeux bruns,*
> *Que je ne sois pas comme l'étang qui s'endort d'un rêve bleu infiniment...*
> *Vous regrettez que je demande encore des roses pour mon front mort...*
> *C'est que je ne puis pas m'en aller où tout repose, sans une caresse et sans remords...*[90]

40

One day about this time I was summoned to the telephone. It was Monsieur Saint-Albert calling from their lakeside hotel. He wanted to make sure we were still there because he was coming to see us. The most I managed to find out about his wife was that she was meant to be coming with him, but had taken another turn for the worse the previous day.

Monsieur Saint-Albert traveled up from below by the cog train immediately after breakfast. Since the room where the Saint-Alberts always used to eat was empty, we sat there to drink our black coffee.

"It gets worse and worse with us," Monsieur Saint-Albert said to me at once.

Seeing me taken aback by this remark, he smiled his winsome smile. But it required even greater effort from him than before.

This time his entire demeanor was markedly constrained. Evidently he had made up his mind, forced himself, to talk about what was most difficult for him.

"It's getting worse and worse between us," he repeated. "Mainly due to my wife's poor health, the state of her heart and nerves," he added by way of explanation. "Despite all my endeavors, despite being prepared to sacrifice my life for her sake—I cannot wrest her from it, cannot save her. I no longer know what to do—that's the situation."

He spoke in all seriousness, eyes cast down, hands clasped around his knees. He didn't find it easy to talk. Long days of anguish, however, had made him decide to do so.

The whole affair had exceeded his powers. It was too great a burden for his youth.

"Would you like me to talk to Madame Saint-Albert?"

Yes, this was precisely what he wanted; he was still counting on my being able to assist him a little somehow.

After a while he said in the same forced tone:

"You'd have thought the death of that man might have ended it, whereas it's precisely the opposite..."

"Death?—Whose death?"

"Ah! Maybe you didn't hear her first husband died recently?"

I recalled having heard something along these lines directly after their departure. And suddenly certain moments in my last conversation with Madame Saint-Albert began to make sense.

"He died, my wife's first husband, my distant relative," Monsieur Saint-Albert reflected out loud in front of me. "So everything has come to an end once and for all, everything is completely finished, *n'est-ce pas*? There's nothing left but the attempt to take your life. She told you as much herself, didn't she? But they saved her again. She's alive. She is still alive, but *he* no longer is. She is sick. The one bad thing is that she's sick. Beyond that however, everything is clear. He no longer exists."

"Meanwhile," he went on, "meanwhile—after he died she wanted to go there at once. However, I put my foot down, I couldn't possibly allow it. So perhaps I myself was the cause, who knows? Her presence in front of the young wife and her two children would have been absolutely out of the question. I don't believe it was just my wounded pride that played a role, my egoism. I could not permit it on any account."

Monsieur Saint-Albert cast his eyes around the glass-paneled room full of flowers, where once upon a time he had perhaps occasionally forgotten his heavy cares.

He pulled himself together however, gathered his thoughts and said with a certain deliberation:

"Her attachment to me, her feelings for me, I do not doubt for a moment. It's the only thing on which I can rely. But she suffered so much in that earlier marriage it's impossible for her to completely forget."

And then after a while he added:

"Small wonder. They loved each other like lovers for fifteen whole years—for fifteen years they were happy. But suddenly he loses his head over a young girl, obtains a divorce and remarries. Not such a rare event, but for a certain type of woman—proud, setting great store by the world's opinion, ultimately respectful of tradition—it can be a very painful blow…"

Thus he strove to set his life in order and come to terms with his misfortune; thus he rendered it possible to accept at any cost—without detriment to his reputation, without erasing a last vestige of hope. And he was so likeable and so helpless in his injured, unappreciated valor and youth, in his superfluous, unwanted feeling.

Because things were quite otherwise and very simple: namely, that despite all the circumstances pointing to the contrary, it was not he who was loved but the one who had died.

41

The very next day I traveled down the valley armed with a bunch of flowers to visit Madame Saint-Albert.

She began by questioning me about life in our villa, about our acquaintances. At first Mademoiselle Hovsepian had come to see her, but not now. Was she ill? They had also not seen Monsieur de Flèche for a long time. And how was little Sossé? And Madame de Carfort, who was so pretty?

I told her who had left and who remained. And that we too were leaving soon. But all this merely indicated Madame Saint-Albert did not wish to talk about herself—now, when I had come expressly for the purpose.

"But Mademoiselle Alice must still be there? How I should like to see her again sometime. What's she up to now?"

I wasn't sure I ought to say anything about Mademoiselle Alice's latest affairs. So I said nothing.

"She had some sort of fears or suspicions about me, quite unfairly. But I always liked her."

Madame Saint-Albert spoke so directly, so carelessly, almost absent-mindedly, I couldn't not believe her. Yes, Mademoiselle Alice—in her restless need for anxiety and danger—had ascribed to herself without any foundation a certain blame surrounding Madame Saint-Albert, suspecting herself of playing some dark role in the affair. Instead, in reality, in relation to its more important aspects—she hadn't even been regarded as a danger.

Conversing, we sat on a large terrace crammed with armchairs upholstered in soft fabrics. It was more like a summer lounge than a terrace. In the corners, above the settees, in the middle of the room, everywhere was chock-full of palms and other green, nonflowering plants. Tall lamps on pillars with soft silk shades promised to transform the place into an evening paradise. A huge awning, let down like a low roof, screened it from the sun. All was dim, stiflingly hot, and rose-hued.

The entire local world was contained within a narrow strip of light between the balustrade and the lower edge of the awning. The mountains, the lake, the green shore—everything was immersed in sunshine against the deep azure of the sky.

"My dear lady," Madame Saint-Albert now spoke unexpectedly. "Do you want to know? I meant to die, because I suddenly grasped that while he was still alive, everything was always possible. I understood life had been possible, because I had always hoped, each and every moment, that I would bump into him somewhere on the highways and byways of the world, and tell him. I hadn't realized before I was living precisely on this sole thought: that I would tell him. Everything I experienced, every day and hour, I would put into words destined only for him. My every agony and craving, my ceaseless craving, my tireless dream of him. I meant to tell him everything. And I told him nothing. He never found out exactly how it was, when I made the decision to go, not to stand in his way, when I myself left when I could have stayed, for surely he would have allowed me ultimately to stay—to remain somewhere nearby and gaze upon their happiness.—Every day I composed wonderful long letters full of entreaties, full of wild folly—and never wrote any of them, because of my foolish pride, because of my fear of seeming ridiculous, because of I no longer know what. Every day I imagined I'd suddenly turn up there, and perhaps strike the very moment when he'd become weary of that other happiness, grown tired of her, and he'd find some small, some last place in his life for me. And I never went..."

Oh, it was a cruel thought that had taken possession of her, and one that was indeed impossible to bear. But there are cruelties we should not inflict upon ourselves, because there's something almost immoral in them.

"Yes, yes," she said. "I could still do everything, while he was alive…"

I looked at her sadly and, if I may put it this way: in indignation. The sight of her anguish was morbid and shameful.

Was she really one of those women, *welche sterben, wenn sie lieben?*[91] Her eyes were sunken. Dark shadows covered her cheeks. Deep furrows stood at the corners of her mouth. She breathed with difficulty. And she did nothing to defend herself against the nightmare. She strode to meet it halfway, beckoning it toward her.

"I want to die. The demand repeats itself within me continually and so solemnly it must surely be real. There's not a thing in the world with which I could counteract it. Not one single value in the world, nothing. Even my most distant memories have turned sour.

"Maybe it was still a function of my youth that I was able to transpose the things and affairs of the world to other places. I tried to force some kind of sense into the stark fact of my grief.

"Now all things have returned to their proper places. It was I who was rejected—and so I lie discarded. There's nothing that could make my suffering important. Nothing has ever told me its truth, as it takes its leave. Nothing has been explained, only everything has come to an end.

"I am dead, totally prepared. How many times have I closed my eyes dreaming: so now I am dying, now I am dead, now…"

42

As we said farewell to that place, the thought occurred to me that it was impossible to distinguish any definite beginning or end in the course of one's life—that nothing can be firmly locked within its own history; that every single thing stretches back to before its beginning and outgrows its end, uniting and interconnecting with other things; that everything in life persists rather than begins or ends.

Because when we arrived, nothing in fact began. Our lives just became intertwined with those of the people already there. And then, when we left, nothing ended either.

Even when someone died, their affairs were not totally wound up and taken care of.

Besides we never found out for sure about Est, if he died or not. If he reached his homeland or not. And yet at the very last moment, as we bade farewell to Madame de Carfort, we spoke precisely of him. I received news of Madame Saint-Albert's death only on returning to our own country. But all she had said to me about old age and about suffering was no less genuine, because of that.

Yes, after that last meeting I did not see her again. On the day we left she was no longer in the hotel but in a nursing home unable to leave her bed.

Everything I'd endeavored to explain to her during our final meeting was naturally of no consequence. And I was convinced of the failure of my mission well in advance.

We announced our departure on our last day at breakfast, and said good-bye to our friends. And those who could not come downstairs we went up to see ourselves.

Signore Costa was long gone, and Carrizales too had left a few days before us. But Miss Norah could still converse in Italian with Signore Vianelli, who seemed far less threatening to her than he had once done to Mademoiselle Alice. And now he too understood her perfectly well, even though she knew barely a few expressions and pronounced them very badly.

Yes, virtually everything was going on just as before. When I took my leave of Miss Norah, I saw nothing had changed at all. People passed through her life, but when they departed, new faces might always arrive to replace them. Her indomitable cheerfulness, her *joie de vivre* which always triumphed over the misery of her disease and the torture of immobility, endured despite everything.

When I went afterwards to say good-bye to little Sossé, Monsieur de Flèche was there once again. He was now so fit he was able to undertake long and difficult expeditions. Just then he was showing her some snapshots of his most recent foray into the mountains—and little Sossé was asking whether she could keep one for herself.

"You've come out really well here," she remarked. And she stared at the little scrap of paper so intently as if Monsieur de Flèche were no longer there beside her.

Mademoiselle Hovsepian also came. She spoke for a moment with little Sossé in Armenian. Among those incomprehensible sounds, I could make out only one, as I could at the beginning: *che, che,* which meant: no.

And I thought to myself in wonderment—as I had at the beginning—that people do not speak to each other in the same way everywhere, unlike the sparrows, who speak to each other in the same way, *che che,* or the amiable chaffinch who sings its song everywhere in the same way, always the same song.

We people like to speak to one another everywhere in a different way—only our laughter and our tears mean the same across the world, comprehensible to anyone.

And yet, when I resided there for several months among people speaking in different tongues, I always sensed we had more in common than not in common. And what we had in common was precisely what was more important—indeed what was the most important.

And the fact that in different locations on earth people make themselves understood through different sounds, have slightly different eye or hair color, slightly different tastes and customs—difference was less important.

But precisely this sufficed for things to be as they are, for there to be misunderstandings between them, hatred, war. And for Mademoiselle Hovsepian to repeat in vain her naive words that one nation should not oppress another.

When we found ourselves alone together for a moment, little Sossé, my dear beloved Sosse who had become such a close
friend, announced quietly, looking me straight in the eye:

"*Madame, je ne vous oublierai jamais.*"[92]

I was about to go, deeply moved by this parting, when she
wanted to tell me something else.

"Did you know that Monsieur de Flèche has agreed to…?"

"What has he agreed to?"

Embarrassed, she explained, smiling her childlike smile:

"He has finally consented to my request, a quite reasonable
one after all. At home, he has a mother waiting for him, and
property that requires management. His presence is needed
there, it's essential. And today he told me at last, that he's reconciled himself…"

"And so he's leaving?"

"Yes, he's leaving. I'm glad he's understood now that he's
well—*n'est-ce pas?*—he ought not to remain here any longer…
Since he's well and has responsibilities down there…"

43

On the morning of our departure, thick, white, wet snow had
fallen on that whole Alpine spring, on the brightly colored flowers, green meadows, trees bursting into bloom.

The world was totally white as we rolled down the mountainside in the little cog train into the abyss of the valley. Through
the carriage windows all the houses, hotels, and villas seemed
lop-sided—as if it were they that had dropped down from somewhere, toppled or keeled over, not we. From the small square in
front of the station, from the road and even from the windows
of our villa, the handkerchiefs were waving as our friends saw us
off in accordance with the local custom.

High above the steep cliff of the gorge, in the white mist of the
snows, a huge flock of birds was circling, gliding and soaring:
the choucas.

But I was thinking of my dearest friend, little Sossé, who wasn't even able to appear at her window. The words of her prayer surfaced in my memory:

Lord, have mercy upon us
Lord, have mercy upon us.
Holy Trinity, send us peace on earth,
Grant health to the sick!
Console the suffering!

APPENDIX
Versions of the Text

The current translation is based on the first book edition (Warsaw, 1927), which is similar to the original 1926 serialized edition in *The Illustrated Weekly* (*Tygodnik Ilustrowany*). A second edition of the novel was published in 1938 by the publisher Książnica-Atlas jointly in Warsaw and interwar Polish Lwów (present-day L'viv, Ukraine), edited and approved by Nałkowska herself. In post-1945 communist Poland, fragments of the novel appeared in an edition of Nałkowska's *Selected Works* (*Pisma wybrane*, 1956) published by the Warsaw publisher Czytelnik. A version of the whole novel was published in 1960, also by Czytelnik, based on the 1926/27 edition, and reprinted in 1980, but with certain fresh omissions (noted in the text). A French translation appeared in 1936 and a Spanish in 1943.[1] As far as I have been able to ascertain, it has not appeared in any other language.

There are various reasons for my choice of edition: a number of problems, associated first with the adjustments made to the text in 1938 by the author herself, and then with censorship procedures in People's Poland, both of which resulted in omissions from the original text, prompted me to return to the original version. I recognize that my decision to use the 1927 rather than the 1938 edition is controversial, since Nałkowska reworked the 1938 text herself and it is the accepted practice to refer to the latest edition of a work published in an author's lifetime. My decision is based on my belief that the 1927 text is a fuller, richer, and more satisfying text.

There are a few places nevertheless where the 1938 edition actually corrects an error in the 1927 edition, or where the tone of the 1927 is softened, resulting in the narrator's voice seeming more distanced or neutral in 1938. An example of the former, is the rendering of Nałkowska's "*cze, cze*" in chapter 1 (the song of the sparrows, which is compared to the speech of one of the Armenian women) as "yes" (Polish "*tak*"), when the Armenian words in fact mean "no, no." While corrected in 1938, the original mistake is included in the 1960 Czytelnik edition, which uses as its basis the earlier edition. An example of the latter—of toning down—would be the description of the narrator's friendship with the Frenchman Monsieur Verdy: in 1927 the narrator asserts directly that hatred of Germans was what "made us brothers to some extent with Monsieur Verdy, we were close because of that hatred," whereas in 1938 this is adjusted to "*in Monsieur Verdy's eyes* we were close because of that hatred" (see chapter 20, italics are mine). In both these cases, and in a few others, I have preferred the 1938 changes. All such departures from my usual adherence to the 1927 edition, as well as significant omissions in the 1938, are recorded in my notes to the text itself. For readers interested in comparing the pre-war Polish editions in detail, a full list of the discrepancies between them may be found in the Editorial Note to the 1980 edition (1980a, 152–53).

Nałkowska's 1938 reworking resulted in several significant omissions which—in my, admittedly subjective, estimation—detract from the original 1927 text, leaving it much the poorer. To give two examples: in chapter 34, there is a long passage describing how the narrator and her companion take a boat out onto Lake Geneva at sunset and row until dark, an event that recalls similar late evening expeditions back home on a lake near Grodno and on other Polish lakes, thus prompting other memories associated with their relationship. Nałkowska excises most of this passage from the 1938 edition, so that the chapter describes only the magnificent sunset and the couple's return to the jetty. The Editorial Note to the 1980 edition claims that Nałkowska's edits to *Choucas* and simultaneously to another novel with similar autobiographical content *House Overlooking the Meadows* (*Dom nad łąkami*) "had one aim: to erase the social distance between the narrator and the people and events described, to remove dispensable sentences that distance the narrator from the cases of individual heroes" (1980a, 151). While it is quite possible Nałkowska wished to reduce the more obviously autobiographical content, there is no real proof that she had any such egalitarian or "socialist realist" intentions regarding her "heroes" (the changes were made in 1938; the editorial note was published under political constraints in 1980). The argument does not hold up, however, when the 1927 and 1938 are compared; many passages are still left in that continue to emphasize the autobiographical associations of the text—in the sense that the text remains, in numerous instances, clearly inspired by personal experience and witness; for example, Nałkowska does not excise in 1938 a reference to that very "house overlooking the meadows" (chapter 19), nor various similar comparisons to things "back home" (the Carnival biscuits called *faworki*, the style of sleighs, types of fence, meadows, and flowers; while in chapter 4 she recalls an edition of *Stories from the Arabian Nights* lying "on a table in my faraway home"). Another significant omission is the long passage from chapter 36 where the Armenian Sossé Papazian relates, in order to explain her theory about the inevitable sufferings of animals, a strange story about a father rat who displays his dead babies to the humans who had killed their mother in a trap.

The most likely explanation for many changes is Nałkowska's constant and almost compulsive need to rework and "correct" her texts, her dissatisfaction and inability to consider anything finished, and lack of belief in her own artistic talent, even a sense that she too easily sacrifices something of herself to please "conventional" expectations. On 6 January 1938, for example, she writes: "These revisions do not bring me the expected pleasure. In the things I wrote, I'm annoyed by what I've not properly captured, by some insignificant flaw in myself. I know I ought to write differently. This nod toward convention and untruth is not great, and yet without it I would be a serious writer" (1988, 280).

The postwar editions of 1960 and 1980, as mentioned above, return to the first edition, restoring almost all the excisions made by the 1938 edition, but ignore the 1938 corrections to previous errors. However, both postwar editions omit a significant paragraph from chapter 8, included in both the 1926/27 and 1938 editions, relating to the establishment of the independent Armenian Republic in the Caucasus in 1918 and its subsequent absorption into the Soviet Union. I include of course this paragraph in the current translation, indicating the place in a note. This act of censorship, however, is not left entirely unmarked: in both 1960 and 1980 the preceding paragraph ends with three dots [...], thus indicating to the alert reader an ellipsis, i.e., that some part of the text had been removed.

NOTE

1. Nalkowska, Sophie. 1936. *Choucas: Roman international.* Traduit par Félicie Wylezynska et Le comte Jacques de France de Tersant. Paris: Société française d'éditions littéraires et techniques; Nalkowska, Sofia R. 1943. *Choucas.* Traducción de Mira Warstacka. Barcelona: Tartessos.

NOTES

1. 1938 edition; the 1927 edition has: "maybe a little smaller than the ones at home."

2. 1927 edition has: "yes," which is corrected by the 1938 edition to "no"; 1960 edition, however, follows the incorrect "yes."

3. Sentence omitted from 1938 edition.

4. Sentence omitted from 1938 edition.

5. Last three sentences omitted from 1938 edition.

6. For the identification of the birds, which strictly speaking are *chocards à bec jaune*, i.e. Alpine chough (*pyrrhocorax graculus*), not *choucas*, see Introduction.

7. *"Dzień dobry, Panu! Jaka piękna pogoda!"* ("Good-day to you, Sir! What beautiful weather!").

8. "Good-day" in Italian. The Polish text has *"buono giorno."*

9. The reference is to Wojski's historic dinner service in Adam Mickiewicz's epic poem *Pan Tadeusz*, Book XII, lines 26–186 (1834). During the course of a banquet, when the patriotic significance of the service and symbolism of the various sweetmeats are explained, the white meringues melt on the plates exposing other kinds of sweet (although Nałkowska refers to the "meringues" as "cream-topping").

10. 1938 edition has "opposite the window."

11. Nałkowska may have been referring to a Polish selection. However, the description of the illustration strongly suggests the edition compiled by Laurence Housman and illustrated by Edmund Dulac, originally published London: Hodder and Stoughton, 1907. The illustration of the Queen of the Ebony Isles is certainly close to Dulac's representation, although it is not embossed on the cover of the original edition. A later mention of Dulac in the novel (chapter 8) suggests that Nałkowska had precisely his illustrations in mind.

12. Sentence omitted from 1938 edition.

13. Blaise Pascal (1623–1662), French mathematician, scientist and philosopher, renowned for his *Pensées* (1669); Joris-Karl Huysmans (1848–1907), French writer, author of the decadent novel *À rebours* (*Against Nature*, 1884); Téodor de Wyzewa (1863–1917), leading French Symbolist of Polish origin (born Teodor Wyżewski), literary critic and writer on Nietzsche; François Mauriac (1885–1970), French novelist, poet, playwright and critic, winner of the Nobel Prize in Literature (1952).

14. *"Do widzenia"* ("Good-bye").

15. "they're sitting at table."

16. "One eats well here all the same."

17. "enough to satisfy their hunger."

18. Phrase removed from 1938 edition.

19. The painter Ivan Aivazovsky (Aivazian) (1817–1900).

20. Sentence removed from the 1938 edition.

21. Or Trabzon (Turkish name) on the Black Sea.

22. Sultan Abdul Hamid II (1842–1918) ascended the throne in 1876 and was deposed in 1909; the reference here is to the Hamidian Massacres 1894–1896. The Young Turk Revolution took place in 1908 and the Adana Massacre in 1909.

23. 1938 edition has instead: "The Turks murdered them everywhere."

24. Phrases "[…] whole armies of ghosts, whole hosts of those destined to die" removed from 1938 edition.

25. Sentence omitted from 1938 edition.

26. The Treaty of San Stefano (3 March 1878) ended the Russo-Turkish War of 1877–1878, and the Congress of Berlin (13 June–13 July 1878) revised the preliminary treaty's provisions.

27. These two paragraphs (from: "In vain…) were omitted from 1938 edition.

28. Now Tbilisi, capital of Georgia. The volunteers joined the Russian imperial army fighting the Ottoman Turks.

29. After the surrender of the Ottoman Empire following defeat in World War I (1918) Cilicia was occupied by the French army and tens of thousands of Armenians were repatriated.

30. Mustafa Kemal Atatürk (1881–1938), founder of the modern Republic of Turkey and its first president.

31. Reference to the Battle of Marash and subsequent genocide of Armenians (January–February 1920) and to similar events in Hadjin (November 1920). The present-day names of Marash and Hadjin are Saimbeyli and Kahramanmaraş respectively.

32. The Republic of Armenia was founded on 28 May 1918 and ceased to exist on 3 December 1920. This paragraph, which appears in both the 1927 and 1938 editions, was censored in the 1960 and 1980 editions published in Poland under communist rule (1945–1989); in 1960, the omission was nevertheless indicated by parentheses containing three dots (...); similarly in 1980, by square brackets [...].

33. The account of early Armenian history here is according to Nałkowska's protagonist. The immediate reference is to the support given to the First Crusade (1096–1099) by the Cilician prince Constantine I. Mazdaism is an alternative term for Zoroastrianism (formed from the name of the Creator Ahura Mazda). Christianity is traditionally claimed to have become the official religion of the then existing Armenian political state in 301. The phrase "as the only Christians at that time in Asia" was omitted from the 1938 edition.

34. The phrase "of its old culture and language" omitted from 1938 edition. Hayastan is the Armenian name for Armenia.

35. This would seem to be a reference to the round church known as Zvartnots, not far from Echmiadzin (Armenia) and dedicated to Saint Gregory, who was credited with converting the Armenians to Christianity and is the patron saint of the Armenian Apostolic Church. The church was built in the mid-7th century and destroyed in the 10th century, most likely by an earthquake. Early in the 11th century, King Gagik I had a round church, closely modeled on Zvartnots, built in Ani. This is a different church again from the ruined Church of Saint Gregory of Tigran Honents, likewise in Ani, completed in 1215, which contains a series of frescoes depicting the Life of Saint Gregory, also known as the Illuminator (c. 257–c. 331).

36. The quotations are from Aram Andonian's edited book *The Memoirs of Naim Bey: Turkish Official Documents Relating to the Deportation*

and Massacres of Armenians, published in English translation (London: Hodder and Stoughton, [1920]), 7–8 and 37–38. Nałkowska's version is very close to this translation, which I draw on here. There is a discrepancy in the final sentence, however. In Nałkowska's version it is rendered as: "The lists of deaths sent to us recently, are not satisfactory." The 1920 English translation has: "The weekly death-rate sent to you during these last few days was not satisfactory." Bab, or Al-Bab, is a district of Aleppo province. Na'im Bey was Chief Secretary of the Deportations Committee of Aleppo. A French translation also appeared in 1920, and is most likely to have been the one encountered by Nałkowska in Leysin: *Documents officiels concernant les massacres arméniens* (Paris: Imprimerie Turabin, 1920).

37. Final phrase omitted from 1938 edition.

38. A play on the first and last line of Francesco Paulo Tosti's (1846–1916) setting of "Chanson de l'Adieu": "*Partir, c'est mourir un peu*" ("To part is to die a little," hence in Est's version: "To die is to part a little").

39. Original 1927, and 1938 and 1960 editions all have: El Cabbalero Andaz [sic]. "El Caballero Audaz" was the pseudonym of journalist, writer and polemicist José María Carretero Novillo (1887–1951). The book mentioned here by Vicente Blasco Ibáñez (1867–1928), the well-known Spanish novelist and Republican, on King Alfonso XIII (*Alfonso XIII desenmascarado*) appeared in French as *Alphonse XIII démasqué: la terreur militariste en Espagne* (Paris: Flammarion, 1924) and in English as *Alfonso XIII Unmasked: The Military Terror in Spain* (New York: Dutton; London: Eveleigh, Nash and Grayson, 1924).

40. El Caballero Audaz's pamphlet was entitled *El novelista que vendió a su patria, o Tartarín, revolucionario (una triste historia de actualidad)* (Madrid: Renacimiento, 1924). A translation appeared in French in 1925 entitled *Tartarin révolutionnaire: la triste histoire actuelle de Blasco Ibáñez* (Paris: [s.n.], 1925); this is most likely the edition seen by Nałkowska. She mentions this work, as well as Ibáñez's book, in her diary (1980b, 165; and Kirchner's notes, 168–69).

41. Miguel Primo de Rivera y Orbaneja (1870–1930), Spanish military leader. He played a major role in Spain's colonial wars in North Africa. In September 1923 he carried out a military coup against Spain's parlia-

mentary government and ruled as dictator 1923–1930. Alfonso XIII sanctioned his actions by appointing him Prime Minister.

42. Sentence omitted from 1938 edition.

43. Phrase omitted from 1938 edition.

44. "It doesn't tire me much." This conversation was omitted from 1938 edition.

45. In 1938 edition the sentence is modified although the sense is more or less the same: "So it was he who supplied the food for the radiators, he who nourished the quivering, vibrating indoor air with warmth."

46. Mohand Abd el-Krim was the leader of the Confederal Republic of the Tribes of the Rif which declared independence from the Spanish occupiers and lasted from September 1921 to May 1926.

47. The Winter Garden.

48. A Spanish stew consisting of assorted meats, fish, and vegetables.

49. Claude Farrère, pseudonym of Frédéric-Charles Bargone (1876–1957), novelist. The reference is most likely to his novel *Fumée d'opium* (1904). When Nałkowska was in Switzerland this was a topical issue, as the Second Opium Conference hosted by the League of Nations was taking place in Geneva (12 January–19 February 1925) aimed at reducing opium trafficking around the world.

50. From the description, this would appear to be the tango.

51. The reference here, and to the apache dance below, is to the Parisian underworld gangs and subculture of this name during the Belle Époque.

52. Floor waiter.

53. The original refers specifically to the Polish traditional carnival-tide or pre-Lenten biscuits known as *faworki*. Moulded into thin twisted ribbons and sprinkled with icing sugar, they are sometimes called in English "angel wings."

54. A reference not to Nałkowska's home with Gorzechowski in Grodno but to Górki, her more permanent parental home near Warsaw, also the inspiration for another novel entitled precisely *House Overlooking the Meadows* (*Dom nad łąkami*).

55. Sentence omitted from 1938 edition.

56. Reference to talks being held at the League of Nations in February 1925 between France and Britain with the general aim of containing German territorial expansion, but where Britain supported certain concessions to Germany opposed by the alliance between France and Poland (1921). Nałkowska briefly mentions this in her diary (1980b, 165).

57. Here, I have preferred the 1938 version. In the 1927 edition, the first part of this sentence reads: "This made us brothers to some extent with Monsieur Verdy."

58. 1938 edition has: "But it was hard to argue about this with Monsieur Verdy, it would have caused him such offence."

59. The daily period of "complete rest" between two and four o'clock in the afternoon was not only prescribed to patients in the sanatoria but was also binding on local people, who had to keep quiet at this time, and was enforced by the police.

60. The four rivers mentioned here are the ones named in Nałkowska's Polish text; it is unclear which river is meant by the "Gail," though it's possible she means "Gihon" or "Gehovn"—it is possible she simply misheard it. The Araxes is also known in English as the Aras. English translations of Genesis 2: 11–14 name the four rivers as the Pishon, Gihon, Tigris, and Euphrates; the Classical Armenian names are similar: Pisovn, Gehovn, Tigris, and Yeprates.

61. The first song included here is omitted from the 1938 edition. The 1938 text has instead the sentence: "When I pressed her, she asked if I would like to hear how an old Armenian sings in exile."

62. This could be a reference to priest, composer, and musician Komitas (1869–1935).

63. This is a close translation of the text as it appears in Nałkowska's Polish original, which she probably transcribed as she remembered it from hearing it in French. The prayer forms part of the Armenian liturgy. In the 2011 translation from Armenian, it is rendered as follows (the line about the "Christian armies" does not appear):

CHOIR: Lord have mercy, Lord have mercy, Lord have mercy, Lord have mercy.

DEACON: Lord have mercy, Lord have mercy, Lord have mercy, Lord have mercy.

CHOIR: O most Holy Trinity, grant peace to the world.

DEACON: And healing to the sick; to those fallen asleep, thy kingdom.

CHOIR: Come O God of our fathers, thou the refuge of those periled.

DEACON: Help thy servants, assist our Armenian people.

CHOIR: Lord have mercy, Lord have mercy, O Saviour Jesus, have mercy upon us.

DEACON: By the mediation of this holy and immortal and life-giving sacrifice.

CHOIR: Receive, Lord, and have mercy.

(*Divine Liturgy of the Armenian Apostolic Church,* translated by Fr Serop Azarian, published by the Armenian diocese of Canada, 2011.)

64. Also known as Abd al-Qadir (1808–1883), Algerian Islamic scholar, military leader and politician; he opposed the French occupation of Algeria in 1830, and was imprisoned in France until released by Napoleon III in 1852.

65. Charles de Foucauld (1858–1916). The 1927, 1938, 1960, and 1980 editions of *Choucas* all spell the name "Foucaud." Considered a martyr, he was beatified by Pope Benedict XVI in 2005.

66. Germany joined the League of Nations on 8 September 1926 and withdrew on 19 October 1933.

67. 1938 edition replaces this phrase with: "of those conquered by their own undertakings, almost at their own invitation."

68. This last paragraph is omitted from the 1938 edition.

69. To crack jokes.

70. 1938 edition has a different sentence: "One can't stand on ceremony in such cases."

71. Panaït Istrati (1884–1935), Romanian novelist.

72. "Switzerland milks its cow and lives peacefully." Line 161 of Victor Hugo's poem "Le Régiment du Baron Madruce" from *La Légende des siècles. Première série XII: Dix-septième siècle—Les Mercenaires,* 1859.

73. Otherwise known as Saint Thérèse of Lisieux (1873–1897). Her spiritual autobiography, first published in 1898, was entitled *The Story of a Soul* (*L'Histoire d'une âme*). I have been unable to find a reference to a Marie Duereux; possibly it appeared in a French contemporary edition. She is not mentioned in the *Bull of Canonization of Saint Thérèse of the Child Jesus and the Holy Face* among the people miraculously cured, allegedly through Thérèse's intercession. Thérèse was canonized on 17 May 1925. Nałkowska left Leysin in April, so this reference must have been inserted retrospectively when she was writing the fictional text.

74. Wilfred Monod (1867–1943) and Leonhard Ragaz (1868–1945), French Protestant and Swiss Reformed respectively, theologians of Christian Socialist persuasion.

75. Previous three lines omitted from 1938 edition; the lines are replaced by the single phrase uttered by Madame Wogdeman, not by the narrator: "I daresay."

76. Acronym for Lenin's secret police founded in December 1917 and known as the Extraordinary Commission for Combatting Counter-revolution and Sabotage (Chrezvychainaia komissiia po bor'be s kontrrevoliutsiei i sabotazhem).

77. Sentence omitted from 1938 edition.

78. "There is no true revolution other than the moral." Georges Duhamel, French writer (1884–1966). The quotation is from his *Entretiens dans le tumulte: chronique contemporaine 1918–1919* (Paris: Mercure de France, 1919, 269). These words from the end of Chapter XLVI are the final words of the book: "*Révolution? Oui! Mais entendez bien: il n'y a de vraie révolution que morale. Tout le reste est misère, sang gaspillé, larmes vaines.*" ("All the rest is misery, squandered blood, vain tears").

79. According to Nałkowska's diary entry (10 April 1925), where she relates a similar incident referring to a Miss Wild who says: "I hate Irishmen," the book in question is *The Middle of the Road* by Philip Hamilton Gibbs (London: Hutchinson, 1922) (1980b, 165; and Kirchner's note, 168).

80. The Château de Chillon; Byron's narrative poem *The Prisoner of Chillon* (1816) was inspired by the story of François de Bonivard, imprisoned in the castle 1530–1536.

81. The remainder of the chapter, except the final paragraph ("Amongst the dark greenery of the gardens…"), is omitted from the 1938 edition.

82. Town in the Podlaskie voivodeship in present-day north-eastern Poland.

83. Gopło is a lake in the present-day Kuyavian-Pomeranian voivodeship in north-central Poland near the historic town of Gniezno. Lakes Białe and Kań are near Grodno, present-day Hrodna in Belarus, where Nałkowska lived with Gorzechowski (see Introduction).

84. Nałkowska's marriage to Gorzechowski did not last; this may have been one reason why she chose to cut the passage in 1938 and this sentence in particular.

85. This paragraph up to this point is omitted from the 1938 edition.

86. This next passage about the rats and the suffering of animals is omitted from the 1938 edition—from and including this sentence to the paragraph beginning: "Throughout all this time, as she spoke, she clutched and rotated the crucifix in her intertwined hands…"

87. The 1938 text resumes the narrative at this point: "As she spoke…"

88. The phrase "he believes in the good" is omitted from the 1938 edition.

89. Possibly a reference to Montreux, given the description of the car journey and meeting with Saint-Albert in chapter 34.

90. "You regret that I have so many frail butterflies in my brown eyes, / That I am not like the pond that falls asleep from a dream infinitely blue… / You regret that I demand more roses for my dead brow… / It's because I cannot depart to where everything reposes, without a caress and without remorse…"

91. "who die, when they love": the last line of Heinrich Heine's poem *Der Asra* (where the line does not refer specifically to women, however, but to a tribe, the Asra). The reference could also be to the title of Carl Schönfeld's 1913 film entitled "…*welche sterben, wenn sie lieben*," starring Friedrich Kayssler.

92. "Madame, I shall never forget you." The last two sentences were omitted from the 1938 edition, perhaps another indication Nałkowska wanted to make the text less personal.

153